TRAIN YOUR
BRAIN

Dr Shireen Stephen holds a PhD in Health Psychology and an MPhil and MSc in Applied Psychology. She is a counselling psychologist, researcher, writer and editor. Well known for her episodic memory of remembering dates and connected events, she is also renowned for her auditory memory of remembering clients and their counselling sessions even years later without taking down any notes! She has also authored *Smart Guide for Awesome Memory* and *The 4-Week Memory Challenge*.

She lives in Bengaluru.

TRAIN YOUR
BRAIN

Ultimate Memory Hacks

Shireen Stephen

RUPA

Published by
Rupa Publications India Pvt. Ltd 2018
7/16, Ansari Road, Daryaganj
New Delhi 110002

Copyright © Shireen Stephen 2018

P-ISBN: 978-93-5304-720-7
E-ISBN: 978-93-5304-762-7

Fifteenth impression 2024

20 19 18 17 16 15

To my daughters Shifrah and Annika,
the original queens at making up riddles and brain games.

Contents

PART II

Chapter 1

Introduction

In 2017, Alex Mullen won the World Memory Championship by memorizing correctly 3,238 random digits in an hour. He won the championship three times in a row!

In 2016, Jonas von Essen recalled 13,208 digits of pi correctly for four hours and forty minutes! He is a two-time world memory champion.

In the 2009 German Memory Championships, Boris Konrad won the gold medal by memorizing 195 names and faces in 15 minutes. He was also able to memorize more than one hundred random dates and events in under five minutes!

In 2006, Andi Bell broke his own record by memorizing a deck of playing cards in 31.16 seconds. He is a three-time world memory champion.

In 2002, Dominic O'Brien entered the Guinness Book of World Records by memorizing a random sequence of 2,808 playing cards (54 packs) after looking at each card only once. He made only eight errors, four of which he was able to correct immediately. He is an eight-time world memory champion!

None of these experts were born with an exceptional memory. In fact, Dominic O'Brien was diagnosed with dyslexia and failed most of his exams in school. Boris Konrad was neither the head of his class, nor did he have the best grades in school. How did all of them get from 'normal' to champions? Simply by training their brains! You too can develop an exceptional memory by training your brain.

Scientists have found that there is absolutely no difference between the brains of memory genius and those of 'ordinary' people. In fact, they performed no better in intelligence tests than 'ordinary' people! The only difference that they found was that memory champions activated numerous parts of their brain when given a problem, whereas 'ordinary' people activated only a few areas of their brain when given the same problem. Dominic O'Brien says, 'A good memory is a reflection of one's ability to make connections between disparate pieces of information by involving *all the functions of the brain*.' The good news is that you can move from ordinary to extraordinary by learning to activate various parts of your brain, just like these memory champions. This can be achieved by stimulating your brain through mental exercises.

Just as your body needs to exercise to become physically stronger, your brain too needs to exercise to become mentally stronger. What happens when you don't exercise your body? You burn fewer calories every day and begin to gain weight, your muscles become soft and weak, your bones may become brittle as you grow older and you tend to fall sick more frequently. Once you start exercising, you burn more calories, lose weight, strengthen your muscles and bones and seldom fall sick. And what's more, even if you stop exercising for a week or two, the health benefits of the exercises still persist. The same is true for your brain. If you don't exercise your brain, the neural connections within your brain begin to get weaker and it becomes difficult to learn new information, concentrate, focus and remember things. Just as with physical exercise, if you stop training your brain for a week or two or even a few months, you will still experience the benefits of the brain training that you had started earlier.

Another common factor between physical and mental exercises is the type of exercise that you do. If you were to run every day for half an hour, you may initially start reducing weight. However, after a few weeks, your body gets used to the exercise and you begin to maintain your weight rather than lose it. In order to continue losing weight, you need to challenge your body by either running for a longer duration or adding other exercises, such as weight training, etc., to your daily routine. In the same way, simply doing the same mental exercises, such as a crossword puzzle every day, is not enough to develop mental training. While you may see an initial improvement in your performance over the first few weeks in terms of the ease or speed at which you can complete a crossword puzzle, this ability stabilizes over time and the puzzles themselves stop being challenging to you. You will then need to either increase the level of difficulty (cryptic crossword) or mix it up with other exercises or puzzles to get the same effect.

In the same vein, just as you may cross-train at the gym by doing cardio exercises, weight training, strength training, focusing on abs, biceps, etc., to get a full-body workout, you need to cross-train with mental exercises to get a full-brain workout. This helps to form new and faster neural connections within the brain, aiding in better memory and concentration and faster grasping of new information. The point is to keep challenging yourself with different exercises that activate different parts of the brain such as creativity, maths skills, language skills, analytic skills, etc.

Physical fitness and mental fitness are directly connected with each other. Physical exercise stimulates your body to release endorphins, the 'good hormones', which elevate your mood. When you are in a better mood, you are naturally more energized and motivated to eat healthier and exercise more, which again improves your physical health. It is, therefore, important to make a lifestyle change to fit in physical as well as mental exercises in your daily routine.

It is never too late to start exercising, both physically and mentally. Dominic O'Brien started mental training at the age of 30, and was already breaking records in a matter of months, while Tony Buzan, who is known as the Master of Memory, began his quest for better memory in college. Studies show that the brains of children as young as two years of age develop more quickly when they are stimulated with games!

Benefits of Brain Training

Brain games force you to think while doing them, challenge you to do old things in new ways, include progressive levels of new learning, require new modes of thinking, involve body-kinaesthetic challenges, are socially interactive and may involve aerobic exercises. These games can involve simple tasks, such as taking up a new hobby to more complex tasks, such as building three dimensional puzzles, learning to play a musical instrument or playing a new sport.

The benefits of brain training are profound in young children as well as adults and senior citizens. In young children, brain training aids in better concentration and reduces hyperactivity. It helps in better cognition (thinking ability), better comprehension of subject matter at school, better reasoning abilities and better creativity and maths skills. Training the brain also boosts productivity, motivation and enhances intelligence and mental flexibility. It aids faster thinking and better reflexes in not only physical activities but in difficult situations which require acumen as well. Studies have shown that when children undergo brain training, the effects can last for up to seven years or more!

In young adults and senior citizens, brain training helps to grasp and solve problems easily, store several items in short-term memory at the same time, and recall names, events and facts quickly. It helps in their ability to see the big picture easily without sorting through the nitty-gritty details and solve problems faster in a stressful situation. Brain games help you think faster, aid in better memory, encourage you to move out of your comfort zone by trying new things, aid your listening skills and observation skills, improve your reaction time so that you can act immediately in any situation, increase your self-confidence and put you in a better mood overall. Brain training reduces the risk of dementia in adults and can improve the memory of people with brain degenerative diseases such as Alzheimer's disease and Parkinson's disease. It can also stave off or slow down the onset of these degenerative diseases.

It is a common myth that your brain degenerates as you grow older. Recent studies have shown that it is not just the *number* of brain cells that you have but the *health* of these brain cells that determine mental decline. The brain is a dynamic organ that continually rewires and adapts itself, even in old age. The miraculous regenerative powers of the brain are seen when new cells develop and also when more connections are made within the neural pathways of the brain. Through brain training, you can keep your brain cells healthy and active throughout your life and even in your old age, by continuously challenging your brain and forming more neural pathways within it. The trick is to include brain training in your daily routine and give it the same importance as physical exercises.

The Routine Brain

Imagine a life where you know exactly what you are going to eat every day, wear every day and do every day. You would not have to think too much on a daily basis since you already know what you are going to eat, wear and do. Your routine would be so predictable that it may actually become boring. Most people go through these 'ruts' every now and then when their lives seem to meander along with nothing really changing and nothing exciting happening. The only way to change this status quo is to shake things up a bit, break from routine and change the predictable patterns in your life.

Routine is a double-edged sword. As you grow older, you may find that life is easier and less stressful when it is predictable. You may then tend to avoid new experiences and develop routines around what you already know and feel comfortable with. In a world where everything is so hectic and stressful, routine can bring stability and peace of mind. However, by following a routine, you may reduce the opportunities for making new associations to an extent that is less than ideal for brain fitness. If things become too predictable, they automatically get boring. It is important to find a balance between necessary routines and predictability so that the mind continues to be challenged. This is where brain games come in.

Brain games help inculcate slight changes in your regular routine to mix things up and are challenging so that you don't continue to do them on auto-pilot. For example, imagine applying toothpaste on your toothbrush and brushing your teeth with your non-dominant hand. Imagine taking a different route to school or work every day, or taking a different modes of transport to school or work. You're still following the routine of brushing your teeth and travelling to school or work, but you've added a touch of novelty to them, which changes the routine a tiny bit and pulls you out of 'auto-pilot mode'.

Since your brain thrives on novelty, the best brain games are those that make you think in new ways. When the brain is presented with non-routine or unexpected experiences, it stimulates more patterns of neural activity which then create more connections between different areas of the brain. This causes the nerve cells to produce more natural brain nutrients which in turn can cause the surrounding cells to become stronger and more resistant to the effects of ageing. Therefore, deliberately breaking from the routine and constantly creating new patterns is a central part of brain training. Making your brain think through how to do a familiar task in a different way forces your memory to exercise in ways which will build and strengthen it.

Another way of strengthening your memory and breaking from the routine is to present your mind with different exercises that challenge it, using skills that you would not otherwise use every day. For example, if you are an English Literature student, you may not use your mathematical skills beyond your everyday transactions. This does not mean that these skills disappear, rather, they may lie dormant and unused while other skills such as creativity, language and comprehension, which are needed to study English Literature are trained and honed. As mentioned earlier, for your memory to develop, you need to be able to activate different areas of your brain. This can be achieved by challenging yourself every day with different games, exercises or puzzles that make use of your analytical skills, language and comprehension skills, logic skills, mathematical skills, creative thinking, spatial skills, etc. By using these skills on a daily basis, you will activate both your left hemisphere and your right hemisphere (sometimes both together) thereby creating more neural connections and enhancing memory, brain health and brain agility.

This book focuses on both types of exercises—those that you can accommodate in your daily routine and those that you will need to make a conscious effort to solve on a daily basis. The key is to proactively shake up your daily routine and/or inculcate brain exercises into your daily schedule so that your brain health increases and the risk of degenerative disorders decrease.

Parameters for Brain Training

The human brain is the most complex organ in the human body. It acts like a storage device which keeps your treasured memories safe, serves you with ample cognitive abilities, influences your personality and regulates your passions and emotions. Since your brain is composed of billions of neural circuits supporting all these functions, exercising just one function such as memory is unlikely to be of much help; rather, a brain fitness program that enhances all these functions and focuses on the overall development of the brain will be of more help. Keeping this in mind, this book focuses on training different types of memory as well as cognitive functions (brain activities) which enhance memory.

This book focuses on different types of memory training—short-term memory, working memory, long-term memory, episodic memory, semantic memory, spatial memory and procedural memory. Cognitive functions that contribute to and enhance memory are processing speed, logic and analytical skills, comprehension, language, numerical reasoning, active observation, lateral thinking, creativity and imagination. These parameters are what standardized intelligence quotient (IQ) tests measure and are scientifically proven to not just improve your IQ but your memory as well.

Short-term Memory is the capacity for holding a small amount of information in your mind in an active, ready state for a short period of time, usually for twenty to thirty seconds. For example, you are making an online transaction and an OTP (one time password) is sent to your phone. You may hold the number in your mind long enough to type it out after which it will be forgotten. It is said that an individual can hold up to seven pieces of information (plus or minus two) in their short-term memory. This may include numbers, names, letters, or any other information.

Since short-term memory helps with the initial stages of taking in new information, learning new information and retrieving information from your long-term memory, it is important to hone this type of memory. The process of developing short-term memory increases attention, concentration and memory span for information.

Working Memory is the ability to actively maintain information in conscious awareness, perform some operation or manipulation with it and produce a result. For example, your friend might give you a telephone number—9011027383—and then say, 'Oops! I think I gave you the wrong number. Just replace the 7 with an 8'. You will then need to go through the whole number again in your mind and make the correction mentally. This number, however, will stay in your mind for the duration that it takes to dial it or write it down, after which it will be forgotten. Working memory involves attention, concentration, mental control and reasoning.

Long-term Memory is the information that is stored in your mind for a long period of time, sometimes for the duration of your entire life! Your long-term memory can virtually hold an unlimited amount of information. This information needs to be encoded in your mind by moving it from your short-term memory to your long-term memory through mindful repetition, rehearsal and association, after which it can be retrieved and remembered at any time. For example, do you remember the name of your very first pet or the model and make of your very first mobile phone? Training your long-term memory will help you remember what you have studied while writing an exam. It will also help you remember dates, events, general knowledge, facts and figures, easily.

Episodic Memory is a type of long-term memory which is autobiographical in nature and helps you remember 'episodes' or events in your life. For example, which movie did you see in the theatre last? What is the gist of the last meeting that you had at work? What did you do last week when your car broke down? Training your episodic memory will help you remember events and experiences in your life more clearly, and will hone your skills of attention, observation and focus.

Semantic Memory is a type of long-term memory which helps you remember general knowledge, facts, ideas and concepts. It is also the memory for the rules of logic that you may use to deduce other facts. For example, if India is in Asia, that means Indians can also be called Asians. Or, if 1 + 2 = 3, then 2 + 1 should also be equal to 3. Training your semantic memory will enhance your general knowledge and broaden your perspective on not just your own life but the world in general.

Procedural Memory is a type of long-term memory for actions which, once acquired, can be performed without much conscious effort. It is the memory that helps you remember how to do something. For example, learning how to skate. Initially, it may require a lot of practice, but once you get the hang of it, you may be able to skate without putting in as much effort or thought. Training your procedural memory helps you hone certain skills such as learning how to swim, playing a musical instrument, riding a cycle, driving a car, tying shoelaces, cooking something for the first time, etc.—things that become much easier with practise.

Spatial Memory is the storage and retrieval of information within the brain that is needed both to plan a route to a desired location and to remember where an object is located or where an event occurred. Finding your way around an environment and remembering where things are within it are crucial everyday processes that rely on spatial memory. For example, while riding a cycle, you would not ride into another vehicle, simply because you know where you are in relation to the other vehicle. This memory is a residual memory that our early ancestors used, to help them avoid predators and be able to come home safe. It is a basic survival instinct that helps you avoid accidents. Training this memory helps better coordination and movement of your body, helps you avoid accidents, learn new routes and remember the locations of objects. It also helps in abstract thinking and in IQ tests and aptitude tests, where you can manipulate the shape and size of an object in your mind to complete a puzzle.

Processing Speed is your ability to quickly scan, discriminate and sequence simple visual information. Exercises in processing speed aid short-term visual memory, attention and visual-motor coordination. The ability to process information quickly is important in exams and aptitude tests. It is also important in everyday life while making decisions and learning new information. Improving processing speed activates the left hemisphere of your brain.

Logic and Analytical Skills are an integral part of developing long-term memory and activates the left hemisphere of the brain while using your working memory. When you understand how things work and why things happen the way that they do, you understand it better and automatically move information from your short-term memory to your long-term memory. It also helps hone your powers of deduction, simply because you understand or learn the cause and effect of things.

Comprehension also aids in long-term memory, because when you understand something, you will remember it for a longer period of time. This is why rote memory or learning things 'by heart' is discouraged. When you learn something by rote, you will remember it for a shorter period of time than when you learn it by understanding it. Comprehension enhances the cognitive functions of the brain and also aids in better concentration and focus. Honing your comprehension skills activates the left hemisphere of the brain.

Language makes use of your working memory and processing speed in terms of manipulating information. Training in language aids in better vocabulary and comprehension and activates the left hemisphere of the brain.

Numerical Reasoning is the ability to grasp relationships among numbers and to understand ideas related to numbers quickly and effectively. By improving this skill, you enhance your ability to solve not only mathematical problems but real-world problems as well since it helps you look at problems critically and analyse them logically. It is directly related to your working memory as well as the left hemisphere of your brain.

Active Observation is the most important skill when it comes to memory and is instrumental in the initial process of taking in information. Observation need not be done by sight alone, but with the use of other senses, such as sound, touch, taste and smell as well. For you to be aware of any information, you need to notice it first. Once you notice it, you encode it in your short-term memory. By actively observing it, you pay more attention to it and move it from your short-term memory to your long-term memory. Active observation then is the key ingredient to awesome memory.

Lateral Thinking activates the right hemisphere of the brain and involves all thought processes that contribute to abstract thinking, creative thinking, problem solving and intuition. When these abilities are trained, you will be able to solve problems quickly and creatively. You will be able to see the bigger picture of events and issues, to think more creatively and 'out-of-the-box', and to understand and develop concepts easily and quickly.

Creativity activates the right hemisphere of the brain and is the ability to create, produce and develop something novel, original and perhaps unexpected. Creativity can be intangible (ideas, theories, jokes, etc.) or tangible (inventions, literary works, paintings, etc.). Creativity is directly connected to memory in the sense that the more creative you are, the better you will remember things. By training this skill, you will not only be training your memory but will also improve your imagination; you will be more innovative, more open to new experiences, willing to experiment with new things and be completely authentic.

Imagination activates the right hemisphere of the brain, and it is the ability of the mind to be creative and resourceful. Imagination is the ability to form images, ideas and sensations in the mind without actually having any sensory input (sight, sound, etc.) from the immediate environment. Imagination can break all boundaries and real-world laws where animals and inanimate objects can talk, people can have more than two arms, legs and eyes, aliens exist, life on other planets are vibrant, etc. Imagination is directly connected to memory in the sense that the better your power of imagination, the better your memory. By training your imagination, you will be able to find creative and imaginative ways to solve problems, apply the knowledge that you have in order to solve issues, learn quickly and easily and expand your thinking capabilities.

Left Brain and Right Brain Functions

As you may have noticed from the parameters listed above, all of them either activate a left brain function or a right brain function.

Both hemispheres of the brain carry out different functions. As already mentioned, to improve memory, you need to be able to activate all the functions in your brain and this can be achieved by exercising both hemispheres of your brain.

The left hemisphere of your brain controls the right-hand side of your body and is the more academic and logical side of your brain. It is in charge of analytical thought, logic, language, reasoning, science and mathematics, number skills and writing skills. This side of your brain is oriented towards detail, facts, comprehension, knowledge and is reality-based and practical. If you use the left hemisphere of your brain more, you may tend to process information in a logical, sequential way. Since the left hemisphere is the seat of language, people who have a left brain preference tend to be strong in verbal logic and reasoning.

The right hemisphere of your brain controls the left side of your body and is the more artistic and creative side of your brain. It is in charge of art awareness, creativity, imagination, intuition, insight, holistic thought, musical awareness and three-dimensional forms (spatial memory). This side of your brain uses feelings, is oriented towards the big picture rather than details, is fantasy based and is instinctive. If you use the right hemisphere of your brain more, your strengths may be visual and spatial reasoning. Since the right hemisphere is the seat of intuition and creativity, people who have a right brain preference tend to process information more intuitively, holistically and randomly.

Brain dominance refers to your thinking and learning preference and is not an absolute. Therefore, the non-dominant part of your brain can be strengthened and trained. The first part of this book contains exercises that will challenge and improve your left brain and right brain functions while the second part contains exercises for both hemispheres that you can incorporate into your daily schedule. This will bring about an overall improvement in not just your memory but in your brain functions as well.

How to Use This Book

Train Your Brain is a guided exercise program that focuses on your mental fitness on a day to day basis. Just as physical cross-training involves different exercises in one session, mental cross-training involves different brain exercises in one session. This will make brain training fun and more effective. This book contains a systematic set of exercises which are carefully designed and sequenced so that your memory and mental efficiency improves.

Studies have shown that in order to cross-train your brain, you need to work on the functions of both your left hemisphere as well as your right hemisphere. A new branch of science called Neurobics focuses on stimulating both hemispheres of the brain. Studies have also shown that relatively brief brain exercise periods that last for less than an hour every day for a week or two can result in significant increases in brain neural networks. This means that all you need is just a week or two to 'jump start' your brain after which you will need to either keep challenging yourself or maintaining the health of your brain with similar or more complex exercises.

Keeping this research in mind, Part 1 of this book provides exercises that will take about 30 to 45 minutes of your time every day for two weeks. On a daily basis, this book provides five exercises that test and train five different parameters of memory. You can either choose to do all five exercises together or space them out through the day. If you feel that five exercises are too much per day and do not want to do them day-wise, you could do just two or three of them as long as you remember to start again where you previously left off.

On a weekly basis, this book provides exercises for two weeks.

The exercises in the first week are beginner- and intermediate-level exercises, while those in the second week are slightly more difficult and are at advanced and expert levels. Since there are about seventeen parameters being tested and trained, the same parameters will repeat twice per week at different levels of difficulty.

Part 2 of this book introduces Neurobics and contains 50 Neurobic exercises that you will be able to incorporate into your daily schedule. Try at least three of these exercises every day but make sure to keep modifying them and not letting the exercises themselves become routine.

The Appendix of this book contains a list of common games such as card games, board games, puzzles, etc., along with the cognitive skills that they help in training. Playing any of these games at least once a week will help train the corresponding cognitive skills.

This book can be used by children and adults alike and is more appropriate for ages 12 and above. It is important to note that exercises that might seem simple to you might be difficult for others. Whether you find the exercises easy or not, try to complete all of them since each exercise trains a different type of memory or cognitive function and is integral in cross-training your brain.

Tips to Train Your Brain

Here are some tips that will help make training your brain more productive and fun.

1. **Have fun.** The whole premise of better memory is to have fun while working your brain. Some of these exercises may be challenging, but use your imagination and creativity and enjoy yourself while doing them.
2. **Relax.** These exercises are not tests. While you may score poorly on some exercises, don't worry too much about

the scores. Instead, use these as challenges to improve that particular aspect of memory.

3. **Challenge your brain.** While you complete these exercises, you will be forming new neural pathways within your brain which will strengthen the neural connections and keep you alert for the rest of the day. Doing these exercises will strengthen your brain and improve your ability to overcome these challenges.

4. **Pace yourself.** These exercises are meant to train your brain, not drain your brain. They will require some amount of energy to solve. If you find yourself fatigued after one or two exercises, stop and take a break.

5. **Don't be too hard on yourself.** Focus more on what you have accomplished rather than what you find difficult. Learn how to solve the difficult problems so that you understand them better and they become less of a challenge for you in the future.

6. **Use mornings effectively.** It is recommended that you 'jump-start' your day with these exercises in the morning so that your brain remains active and agile through the day. You may learn a memory trick or two which you can then practice through the day.

7. **Transfer learning.** While it is enough to simply work out mental exercises every day, you can enhance your memory by transferring these games to your daily life. For example, if you have just learnt a new technique to remember numbers, why not test it when you go out by trying to remember the licence plate numbers of vehicles that you see on the road? Training your memory does not begin and end with this book—you need to transfer it to everything else that you do.

8. **Think long term.** While this book provides you with

exercises for two weeks, the effects of this brain training will last a few months. Continue the process beyond two weeks by solving any puzzles or exercises that you can get your hands on. Daily newspapers are a good place to start. Keep in mind that brain training needs to be a life-long endeavour.

9. **Hands on.** While some exercises might be brain teasers and riddles that don't require much beyond your thinking capabilities, other exercises may require you to write them down in order to work them out. Keep a pen and paper handy.

10. **Reward yourself.** After completing your workout for the day or the week, reward yourself with something that you like. It can be something as small as taking a 'music break' to listen to your favourite music, to eating something that you really like, to just patting yourself on the back. You've earned it!

Disclaimer: Achieving a measurable improvement in your memory requires dedication and commitment on your part. Improvement does not just happen overnight. You will have to put in the effort to achieve maximum results.

SUMMARY

- The only difference between your brain and the brain of a memory champion is that a memory champion activates and uses more functions in his or her brain. You can learn to activate all parts of your brain through brain training.
- Just as physical exercise makes your body stronger, mental exercises also make your memory sharper and stronger.

- Brain training can reduce the risk of degenerative diseases such as Alzheimer's and Parkinson's disease. It can also delay the onset of these diseases.
- Brain training involves breaking from routine. It also involves different exercises that will train different cognitive functions performed by the left hemisphere and the right hemisphere of your brain.
- This book focuses on training different types of memory as well as cognitive functions, such as processing speed, creativity, logic and analytical skills, etc., that are directly connected to memory.
- Have fun while doing the exercises. Try and complete all five exercises every day.

Chapter 2

Principles of Memory and Memory Techniques

Before starting with brain training, it is important to keep certain principles of memory in mind. These principles will not only aid your memory but will also help you with the exercises in this book.

Ten Principles of Memory

1. **Interest**: Interest plays an integral part in learning new things. You automatically learn better when you are interested in something, but your motivation goes down when you are disinterested. While doing these exercises, take interest in them and work them out, even the ones that you are unfamiliar with.

2. **Association**: We always learn something new by relating it to or associating it with something that we already know. For example, the game Kakuro might seem new to you, but there is only one difference between Sudoku and Kakuro. If you are aware of the rules of Sudoku, you will be able to apply the techniques that you use to solve a Sudoku puzzle on the Kakuro puzzle and win, even though you have never attempted the latter before. Associating new information to information that you already know forms the basis of memory since learning anything new depends on this principle. While doing the exercises in this book, try and actively associate the information within the exercises so that you will remember them better.

3. **Visualization**: Visualization is a powerful memory principle

that helps you conjure up pictures in your mind. Your mind has the capacity to remember an unlimited number of visual images, and therefore, when you convert what you are reading into a mental picture, you will remember it better. If you are reading a story, 'see' it like a movie in your mind. If you are working with numbers, try and convert them into mental images that will 'stick' better in your mind. Your mind will automatically remember the images which you can then convert back into numbers. Use all your senses to create vivid and colourful pictures. While working out the exercises in this book, try and convert them into pictures in your mind as much as possible.

4. **Imagination**: Use your imagination to make learning anything new fun and enjoyable. Your imagination has no boundaries. Unleash it in your mind to make mental images as outrageous as possible, as ridiculous as possible and as funny as possible. Exaggerate the images, make them look like cartoons or caricatures in your mind and be as rude as you like. You tend to remember things that are out of the ordinary, outrageous, ridiculous, fun, exaggerated and rude better than you would ordinary things. The trick is to make ordinary things extraordinary in your mind. While doing the exercises in this book, first have a mental image. Next, make this mental image as ridiculous as possible. You will see an immediate increase in your ability to recall new information!

5. **Active observation**: People often limit observation to something that you can see with your eyes, but it is much more than that. Active observation involves using all your senses of touch, sound, sight, taste and smell to be more aware of your environment and what is happening to you and around you. Observation is the first step in memorizing anything because it is at this stage that information enters

your awareness after which it travels to your brain where it is interpreted and stored or forgotten. When you actively observe things around you, you are more aware of the information that you are paying attention to and your brain will automatically store this information rather than forget it. Some of the exercises in this book require you to actively observe information within them in order to solve them. These exercises may also require you to observe things in your home or your environment. Make sure to use all your senses while attempting them.

6. **Chunking**: It refers to the breaking up of big pieces of information into smaller groups of information that are easier to process. These smaller groups of information are called chunks. From the age of 15 onwards, you will be able remember about seven bits of information—plus or minus two—using your untrained memory. That means, if a phone number is ten digits long, you will be able to remember about 5 to 9 digits without using memory techniques. However, if the phone number is chunked into groups of numbers like 555-851-2458, you may be able to remember it better. The interesting thing about chunking is that while you can remember seven chunks easily, you can also remember up to seven items under each chunk as easily. This means that you can remember up to 49 pieces of information effortlessly, without using memory techniques! While working out some of the exercises in this book, try and chunk the information into smaller pieces. This will help you work with them easily and remember them better.

7. **Patterns**: Your brain is already tuned to recognise patterns in large pieces of information. For example, look at the following letters for 20 seconds and then close the book and write them down:

C N N A B C C B S M T V F O X N B C B B C

Could you remember all of them? If not, try and find patterns in them. By chunking them into groups of three, you now get:

CNN ABC CBS MTV FOX NBC BBC

By recognizing that these seemingly random letters are actually the names of television channels, do you think you could remember them better? Always look for patterns in anything that you do. When it comes to brain training exercises, pattern recognition is important, especially when training spatial memory, abstract reasoning and creativity.

8. **Big and Little Pictures**: This is sometimes referred to as seeing the forest *and* the trees. If you focus only on the forest, you miss the beauty of individual trees. If you see only the individual trees, you miss seeing how all the trees together make up a large forest. The memory principle of big and little pictures is a process of identifying different levels of information from large concepts, themes and ideas to smaller details such as facts, definitions, examples, data, etc. Both higher and lower levels of information are important in the learning process. Some of the puzzles in this book such as sudoku and kakuro require you to not only look at the bigger picture but its components as well.

9. **Concentration**: This is the ability to block out distractions in order to stay focused on one specific item or task. Needless to say, when you focus and concentrate on one task, you will remember it better. The exercises in this book require your attention and concentration for less than 45 minutes every day. Even if you space out your exercises through the day, try and do them in an environment that has very few or no

distractions so that you can concentrate better.

10. **Ongoing Review**: While information stays in long-term memory on a relatively permanent basis, it begins fading with time if it is not reviewed occasionally. Ongoing review is a crucial step in the learning process as it helps cement information in your long-term memory. Even after completing all the exercises in this book, try and find similar exercises in daily newspapers, magazines, etc., so that the processes that you use to complete these exercises get cemented in your mind. This will increase the benefits of brain training to last anywhere from a few months to a few years!

Memory Techniques and Mnemonics

A good memory is a skill that can be learnt like any other skill and at any age. However good your memory is now and whatever age you are, you can improve your memory substantially by using the techniques outlined in this chapter. This section provides you with a brief overview of some memory techniques and mnemonics that will be useful for you while doing the exercises in this book. Take time to learn and practice some of these techniques before you start on the exercises and then stick with the ones that work best for you. Also, keep in mind that while it may take a few pages to describe these techniques, it only takes a few seconds for you to put them into action. Once put into action though, these strategies produce almost immediate results in boosting your mental agility as they use the natural processes of your brain and work *with* your brain, not against it.

Let's take a list of ten random words to learn how different memory techniques can be applied to the same information. These same ten words will be used for all the techniques described in this section. The words are:

Elephant, lantern, eraser, cone, telephone, wine,
horse, ice cream, number, eye

Acronyms and Acrostics

Acronyms and acrostics are a great way to remember lists of items in the correct order. With acronyms, the first letters of each word to be remembered may (or may not) form another word. For example, UFO (**U**nidentified **F**lying **O**bject), NASA (**N**ational **A**eronautics and **S**pace **A**dministration), ET (**E**xtra-**t**errestrial), etc. With acrostics, the first letters of each word to be remembered are made into another more memorable sentence or phrase. For example, the phrase 'Large Mean Monkeys Jumped Very Slowly Down' signifies the days of the week in French starting from Monday—*Lundi, Mardi, Mercredi, Jeudi, Vendredi, Samedi* and *Dimanche*. By remembering this phrase, you will remember the first letters of the days of the week and that will act as a clue for you to remember the words.

While attempting brain training exercises, you may be asked to memorize a group of words in a limited time frame and write them down. For these exercises, it may help to make up an acronym or an acrostic on the spot so that you can remember them quickly. If you were to make an acronym with the ten words listed above, you will get—ELECTWHINE or **ELECT WHINE**. Using these letters, you can make up an acrostic—Emily Left England Continuing To Washington High, In New Equipment.

Do note that the acrostic does not have to be factually correct. As long as it aids you in remembering the words that you need to memorize, it does not matter what words you use. Also keep in mind that while acronyms and acrostics act as memory aids, they will not help you unless you know the words to begin with. If you forget 'elephant, lantern, eraser, etc.', all you will be left with is the first letters of ELECT WHINE but not what they stand for.

Rhymes and Music

Rhyming anything that you would like to study will imprint it in your mind and you will remember it for a longer time. Making up a song or putting new information to music will also help in remembering things better. For example, if you want to remember that your car is parked in sub-basement 4, row 33 at the mall, you can make up a silly rhyme that you can then put to music. It may go something like this:

I know,
My car is in **sub-basement four**,
Row thirty-three
Is where it will be!

Even if you spend all day at the mall, you will still be able to remember where your car is parked simply by recalling this rhyme. When working out the brain exercises in this book, try and rhyme the words to be remembered or put them to music. Using the ten words listed above, you can make up a silly rhyme:

Elephant, lantern, eraser, cone,
All sat by the **telephone,**
Drinking **wine** with the **horse,**
Which was nice of course,
Except for the **ice cream**, the **number** and **eye.**

Pure Links

Just as links on a chain are connected, you can link any information together. Seemingly random or unconnected words can be linked together by forging a connection and giving them some meaning. This technique makes use of your association skills and your visualization skills to form vivid associations and mental pictures of the data that you are linking. You may need to practice this skill of linking to such an extent that when you look at a list of words, linking images should pop into your mind immediately!

Now, take the list of words mentioned earlier—*elephant, lantern, eraser, cone, telephone, wine, horse, ice cream, number, eye*—and start linking the first and second word, the second and third word, the third and fourth word and so on. When you move on to the second pair of words, the first word has to be 'dropped'. Use the principles of memory to make the associations as ridiculous, silly and outrageous as possible. See these images clearly in your mind.

We'll start with the first pair of words—elephant and lantern. Imagine an elephant marching, holding a lantern with his trunk. Now drop the word elephant and move on to the next pair of words.

Lantern and eraser: Imagine a lantern quickly trying to erase itself before it is seen and captured!
Eraser and cone: An eraser in the shape of a cone.
Cone and telephone: A cone hopping on a telephone keypad trying to dial a number.
Telephone and wine: A telephone gobbling down some wine.

Try and work out the rest yourself:

Wine and horse: ————————————————————
Horse and ice cream: ————————————————————
Ice cream and number: ————————————————————
Number and eye: ————————————————————

Now close your eyes and try and recall all the words beginning with elephant. Did you get them all correct? Close your eyes again and try and remember all the words in reverse order starting with eye and linking your way backwards. How did you do this time?

If you were not able to remember a word, it could be because the images that you formed or the links that you made were not vivid enough, strong enough or memorable enough. This technique takes some practice but once you master it, you will be creating the most vivid, outrageous pictures in your mind effortlessly.

While working out some of the exercises in this book, you may need to link information in order to remember everything. This method will come handy.

Story Link

A story link is the most common method to remember a list of words and is the easiest to use. Simply use the words to be remembered in the same order that they need to be remembered and make up a ridiculous story with them. It can be something like this:

> An **elephant** bumped into a **lantern**, dropping its **eraser** and its **cone**. It went to a **telephone** booth nearby to call for some **wine** to drink and its **horse** to take him home. On the way, it stopped for **ice cream** but was given the wrong token **number** which it **eyed** with annoyance.

When working with unconnected words, try and connect them by using either pure links or story links.

Number Shapes

If you have problems remembering numbers, this method is for you. Think of objects that have a similar shape to each number from 0 to 10 and picture it clearly in your mind. For example, the number 0 might look like a donut, the number 1 might look like a candle, the number 2 might look like a duck, etc. Once you have the number shapes clearly in your mind, you can start associating them with anything that you would like to remember in the correct order. Here are some possible number shapes.

0 – Donut

1 – Candle

2 – Duck

3 – Heart on its side

4 – Sailboat with open sails

5 – A seahorse facing right

6 – An elephant's trunk

7 – A candy cane

8 – A snowman

9 – A tennis racket

10 – A girl holding a hula hoop

You need to have these images firmly in your mind as you can use them over and over again to remember anything. For example, you get a new debit card and you need to remember the new PIN number that the bank has sent you—8290—which translates to snowman, duck, tennis racket and donut. Using the story link, make up a short story—

> A **snowman** and a **duck** throw their **tennis rackets** around while eating **donuts**.

If you have this story in your mind, you will not forget your new PIN number!

Now, let's see how to remember lists with this method. Pair each number to each word listed above and make simple associations with them. Note that you need to pair each number with each word. You do not need to 'drop' a word as you do in the link system as each image will automatically tell you the number associated with the word to be remembered.

1.   Candle and elephant: Imagine a candle shaped like an elephant.

2.   Duck and lantern: Imagine a duck carrying a lantern

and waddling around in the dark.

3. Heart and eraser: I love erasers!
4. Sailboat and cone: Imagine a toy sailboat sailing round and round on a conical bucket.

   Try and work out the rest yourself.
5. Seahorse and telephone:———————————
6. Elephant trunk and wine:———————————
7. Candy cane and horse: ———————————
8. Snowman and ice cream: ———————————
9. Tennis racket and number: ———————————
10. Girl with hula hoop and eye: ———————————

Now if you want to remember what the second word was on the list, you think of the shape for number 2 which is duck. What was the duck doing? It was waddling around in the dark carrying a lantern. Right! The second word was lantern! In the same way, you will be able to remember the entire list just by remembering the images for the numbers and what they were 'doing'.

When doing number exercises in this book, quickly convert the numbers into images and you will remember them better.

Alphabet Tags

You can use alphabet tags in the same way that you used number shapes. For this, you need to go back to your pre-school days and remember the alphabet song and what words are associated with each letter of the alphabet. For example, A for apple, B for ball, C for cat, etc. Write them all down. Now, using the same method as the letter shapes, you can use these tags to remember any information that you want. Using the same list of words above, you can tag each word to each consecutive letter of the alphabet like so:

Apple and elephant: Imagine an apple falling on an elephant's head and bouncing off!

Ball and lantern: Imagine a ball falling into a lantern and catching fire.

Cat and eraser: Imagine a cat batting around an eraser with its paws.

Continue on with your own set of words/images for each letter of the alphabet and associate them with the rest of the words in the list above. Once you are done, close your eyes and start at A and move to J and see if you can remember all the words in their correct order.

As you can see, different techniques can be used to memorize the same type of information, so it definitely pays to know at least one or two of these techniques thoroughly. Learning the link system and story links will help you remember long lists of words however, if your associations are not strong enough, the link can easily be broken and you may find it difficult to remember the next item on the list. Number shapes help you convert numbers to more memorable images and remember a short list of items while alphabet tags help you convert random letters to memorable images while aiding you in remembering longer lists.

SUMMARY

- The ten principles of memory include interest, association, visualization, imagination, active observation, chunking, pattern, big and little picture, concentration and ongoing review. These principles not only aid your memory but will help you with the exercises in this book as well.

- Memory mnemonics include acronyms, acrostics, rhymes and music.

- Acronyms are words formed with the initial letters of words that need to be remembered.
- Acrostics are sentences formed with the initial letters of words that need to be remembered.
- Making a rhyme out of anything that you need to remember or putting it to music will aid your memory.
- Linking words on a list together through some ridiculous association will help you remember all the words on the list.
- Story links use all the words in the same order in the form of a story.
- Number shapes convert numbers into more memorable images. You can then use these images to remember information by associating them with the information.
- Alphabet pegs convert the letters of the alphabet into more memorable images by using the words and images already associated with the letters. You can then use these images to remember longer lists of information.

PART I

Chapter 3

Week 1—Day 1

Are you ready to start training your brain? Let's begin! As mentioned in Chapter 1, you will have five exercises each day, which will take about thirty to forty-five minutes to complete. Try and do them all in the morning but if this is not possible, try and pace them through the day with two in the morning, two in the afternoon and one at night. All exercises will test and train the same parameters as mentioned in Chapter 1.

A hint is provided at the end of some exercises. Try the exercise first by choosing any method you like. Once you finish, read the hint and try the exercise again with the suggested method. This is a good way to check the effectiveness of memory methods and mnemonics.

Today's focus is on short-term memory, working memory, long-term memory, episodic memory and semantic memory.

Exercise 1: Random Words

Focus: Short-term Memory
Time: 2 minutes
Materials required: Paper and pen/pencil
Level: Beginner's

Study the following list of ten words for two minutes, then close the book and write them down.

chocolate	paper
compass	flower

hair clip	window
chalk	car
bubbles	sparrows

Hint: Use Pure Links, Story Links or Acronyms methods.

Scoring: 10 points for every correct answer.
Your Score: ─────────────────────

Exercise 2: Reverse Numbers

Focus: Working Memory
Time: 4 minutes
Materials required: Paper and pen/pencil
Level: Beginner's

Read the following rows of numbers. Take only 15 seconds per row, then close the book and write them down *in reverse*. For example, if the number is 337, you need to write it down as 733. To make this exercise a bit tougher, you can ask somebody to read out the numbers to you. As soon as the person finishes calling out the numbers in the first row, write them down in reverse. Ready? Go!

18339
382924
9173848
70283945
750383047
3826492749
182794737927
222999333888111

Hint: Try chunking the numbers into groups of three or four. Read the chunks, not in terms of individual numbers, such as one-three-five, but rather as a whole number such as one hundred and thirty-five.

Scoring: 10 points for every correct row.

Minus 5 points for every wrong row.

Your Score:————————————————

Exercise 3: Animal Babies Crossword

Focus: Long-term Memory
Time: 10 minutes
Materials required: Pen/pencil
Level: Beginner's

Work out the following crossword puzzle on animals and their babies, taking no more than 10 minutes. Since the answers are already in your long-term memory, you need only recall them.

Hint: If you do not know an answer, ask somebody for it or Google it rather than checking the answer at the back of the book. This will help store the information in your long-term memory.

Across	**Down**
1. Animal that burrows underground	1. Baby fly
3. Baby dog	2. Baby alpaca
5. Baby goose	4. Cat sound
8. Baby mosquito	6. Baby pigeon
9. Baby cow	7. Baby alligator
11. Natural home or environment of an animal (abbreviation)	9. Baby elephants (plural)
12. What you find in aquariums	10. Baby deer
13. Nocturnal bird	12. What 12 across breathes with
14. What octopi shoot out	
15. What clucks	
16. Baby duck	

Exercise 4: Recall Quiz

Focus: Episodic Memory
Time: 10 minutes
Level: Beginner's

Find a quiet place where you can shut your eyes and take yourself back in time. Try to recall each scene with as much detail as possible.

Answer the following questions.

1. What did you eat for breakfast last Saturday?
2. When and where was the last time you had an ice cream?
3. Which movie did you watch last in the theatre?
4. Can you remember the last time you felt really happy?
5. How did you celebrate your tenth birthday?
6. What did you do on the last day of your final exams?

7. Who was your class teacher in kindergarten?
8. What was the naughtiest thing you did as a child?
9. Who was your first crush?
10. Is there something about you that only you know but nobody else does?

Exercise 5: General Knowledge Quiz

Focus: Semantic Memory
Time: 10 minutes
Materials required: Pen/pencil
Level: Beginner's

Answer the following questions.

1. What is the area around the North Pole called?
   a) The Antarctic
   b) The Arctic
   c) Alaska

2. What is the slowest-moving land animal?
   a) Three-toed sloth
   b) Garden snail
   c) Tortoise

3. How many eyes does a Cyclops have?
   a) Three
   b) One
   c) Four

4. Which blood cells are responsible for delivering oxygen around the body?
   a) White blood cells
   b) Red blood cells
   c) Blue blood cells

5. What is the world's biggest hot desert?
   a) Gobi
   b) Arabian
   c) Sahara

6. How many wives did King Henry VIII have?
   a) Eight
   b) Five
   c) Six

7. Which country has the longest coastline?
   a) Australia
   b) Canada
   c) India

8. When the tide 'ebbs' what is happening to it?
   a) It drains away
   b) It rises again
   c) It is staying constant

9. What is the smallest insect?
   a) Fairyfly
   b) Mayfly
   c) Fruit fly

10. Which of these was invented by Benjamin Franklin?
    a) Compass
    b) Bunsen Burner
    c) Bifocals

Scoring: 10 points for every correct answer.
Your Score:————————————————

Exercise of the Day

Spend a minimum of fifteen minutes today in physical exercise. It can be a fifteen-minute walk, jog, run or swim; or it could be cardio exercises, weight training, aerobics or Zumba. Any physical exercise is fine, as long as your body gets a workout.

Looking ahead: To prepare yourself for tomorrow's exercises, make sure you have the following ingredients at home. Instant coffee powder, sugar, full cream milk, ice cubes and chocolate syrup (optional).

Chapter 4

Week 1—Day 2

Today's focus is on procedural memory, spatial memory, processing speed, logic and analytical skills.

Exercise 1: Cold Coffee Milkshake

Focus: Procedural Memory
Time: 15 minutes
Materials required: Instant coffee, warm water, sugar, milk, ice cubes and chocolate syrup
Level: Beginner's

Procedural memory is the part of your memory that tells you how to do things. It also helps you build specific skillsets. Today's focus will be on following a recipe. If you choose to not follow the recipe, spend fifteen minutes instead practising a musical instrument or pursuing a hobby that you are interested in.

Here is the recipe for a cold coffee milkshake. At first, you will need to follow the directions of the recipe, but if you make this delicious drink often enough, you will be able to make it without consulting the recipe at all!

Ingredients:

- 1 tablespoon instant coffee powder
- ¼ cup warm water
- 3–4 tablespoons sugar (or as required)
- 2 cups chilled full-cream milk

- 6–8 ice cubes (or as required)
- Dash of chocolate syrup (optional)

Recipe:

- In a blender, mix the instant coffee, sugar and water.
- Blend for a minute or till the coffee solution becomes frothy and the colour lightens.
- Add the ice cubes and the milk.
- Blend once more till everything is mixed well and you get a nice froth on top.
- *Optional*—Line the mug/glass with chocolate syrup before pouring the coffee into it.
- Serve cold.

Exercise 2: Spatial Puzzles

Focus: Spatial Memory
Time: 2 minutes
Materials required: Pen/pencil
Level: Beginner's

Spatial memory is the ability to manipulate figures and shapes in your mind and find the answers to abstract questions. Test and hone your spatial memory by answering the questions below.

1. Which cube *cannot* be made based on the unfolded cube?

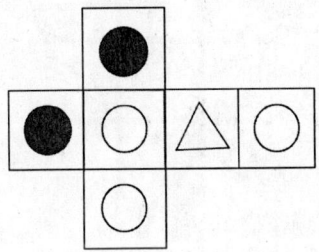

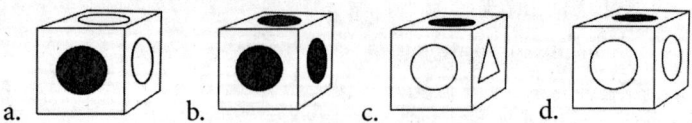

a.　　　b.　　　c.　　　d.

2. What is the mirror image of the image below?

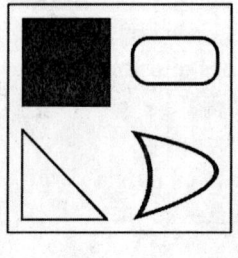

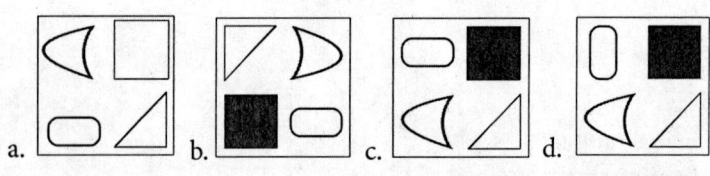

a.　　　b.　　　c.　　　d.

3. In a game of tic tac toe/knots and crosses, your opponent is X, while you are O. Your opponent has played twice, and it is your turn now. Where should you place your next O to win? *Note: You need to get three Os in a row, either horizontally, vertically or diagonally to win.*

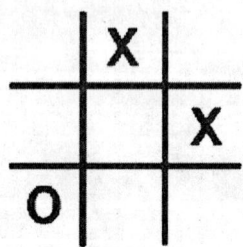

a) Middle square
b) Either upper left corner or lower right corner
c) Upper right corner
d) Either middle row left square or bottom row middle square

4. Which of the lines between the arrowheads is the longest?

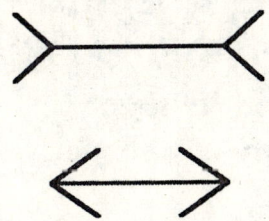

5. A piece of metal is placed in a plastic bowl that floats in a bath full of water. The metal is then taken out of the bowl and dropped in the water. Does the water level rise, fall or remain the same?

Exercise 3: Up-Down-Left-Right

Focus: Processing Speed
Time: 5 minutes
Level: Beginner's

Look at the image below and call out the directions to which the arrows are pointing as quickly as you can (left, right, up, down). Start with the first row and move to the second row, etc., till you reach the last row. Time yourself. Once you are done, take a break for ten seconds or so and redo this exercise and try and beat your time. Do this at least five times till you get your best score.

→	↑	←	→	↓	↑	↓	↑
↓	→	→	←	→	←	↑	→
↑	←	↓	→	↑	→	↓	←
→	↓	↑	↑	↓	→	→	↓
←	↑	→	↓	←	↓	←	↑
↑	↓	←	↑	↑	↑	↑	→
→	←	↑	→	→	←	↓	→
↓	→	→	↓	↑	↓	→	←

Time 1:————————

Time 2:————————

Time 3:————————

Time 4:————————

Time 5:————————

Exercise 4: Just Deduce It!

Focus: Logic
Time: 3 minutes
Materials required: Paper and pen/pencil
Level: Beginner's

Logical skills are your ability to deduce answers from given clues. Read the following questions and see how quickly you can deduce the correct answers.

1. Mary, Elizabeth and Sarah are three sisters. Which of them is the youngest?
   a) Mary is the oldest.
   b) Elizabeth is not the oldest.
   c) Sarah is not the youngest.

2. Merlin realizes that all Alakazams are Open Sesame, and some Hocus Pocus are Alakazams. Is it true that some Hocus Pocus are Open Sesame?
   a) True

b) False

3. Five friends are trying to see who is the tallest. Asha is taller than Sahana but shorter than Smriti. Debbie is taller than Nancy but shorter than Asha. Who is the tallest?
   a) Asha
   b) Sahana
   c) Smriti
   d) Debbie
   e) Nancy

4. Mark is standing behind Luke but at the same time, Luke is standing behind Mark. How is this possible?

5. When Ann had her birthday in the year 2000, she became 8 years old. However, she was born in the year 2008. How can you explain this?

Exercise 5: Riddle Me This

Focus: Analytical Skills
Time: 5 minutes
Level: Beginner's

Analytical skills tests your ability to analyse a problem and form logical conclusions. Read the following riddles, and try and deduce the correct answer.

1. A woman was in her hotel room when there was a knock on the door. When she opened it, she saw a stranger. He looked surprised and said, 'I'm sorry, I thought this was my room!' He then left and walked towards the elevators. The woman, however, locked her door and then dialled security. Why was she so suspicious?

2. A man is found dead at the bottom of a multi-storey

building. Seeing the position of the body, it is evident that he jumped from the window on the top floor. Inspector Narayan first goes to the first floor and walks to the window facing the direction in which the man was found. He opens the window and flips a coin through it, watching it as it lands. He then goes to the second floor and repeats the process. He keeps on doing it till the top floor, after which he deems it a murder and not a suicide. How does he know?

3. In the year 2000, a 40-year-old doctor told his son that when he was a little boy, he decided to become a doctor after seeing a puppy undergo a heart transplant on a website. He then thought that he would become a doctor so that he could help people in a similar way. What is the defect in this story?

4. A man placed a $100 dollar bill on his desk and left for work. When he returned home that evening, the money was gone. He had three suspects: the cook, the maid and the plumber.

    The cook said she put the bill between pages 5 and 6 of a book on his desk to keep it safe. The man checked and it was not there.

    The maid said she saw the bill sticking out of the book and placed it between pages 1 and 2 while she was cleaning. Again, the man checked the book and there was nothing between pages 1 and 2.

    The plumber said he saw the bill sticking out of the book and he moved it between page 4 and 5 to keep it safe. Again, the man checked but found nothing.

    Who stole the money?

5. The Petersons had reported a robbery. 'All my wife's jewels are missing. You'll want to check inside for fingerprints,' Mr Peterson said to the policeman, pointing to the broken window glass on the lawn. The burglar presumably entered the house by breaking through the window. The policeman noticed that the room had a number of very tiny pieces of window glass particles scattered around near the broken window area and replied, 'That won't be necessary. There's been no burglary.' What made the policeman so sure?

Exercise of the Day

Spend a minimum of fifteen minutes today practising a musical instrument. If you do not play any musical instrument, spend some time with a hobby of your choice.

Chapter 5

Week 1—Day 3

Today's focus is on comprehension, language, numerical reasoning, active observation and conceptual thinking.

Exercise 1: The Naughty Elf

Focus: Comprehension
Time: 10 minutes
Materials required: Pen/pencil
Level: Beginner's

Read the following passage only once and then answer the questions that follow. Once you finish reading the passage, cover it up while answering the questions.

When Mrs Johnson's students got to school this morning, they found a big surprise waiting for them in class. All the chairs were upside down and under the tables, the posters in class had been ripped off the walls, turned back to front and pinned back on and there was water all over the floor! A naughty elf had come in sometime during the night and had messed up the whole classroom! As they continued walking through their class, they found more and more strange things. There was a gold fish swimming around in the water cooler, there was green glitter on the ceiling and all their coloured chalk had been replaced with black chalk! Imagine writing on a black board with black chalk! They also found that all their stationery was missing and that the names on their desks had been mixed up. The elf sure had been naughty!

1. What is the class teacher's name?
2. What was the first thing that the students noticed upon entering the class?
3. What had happened to the posters on the wall?
4. When had the naughty elf come in?
5. What were the strange things that the elf had done to the classroom?

Exercise 2: Word Circles

Focus: Language
Time: 5 minutes
Materials required: Pen/pencil
Level: Beginner's

Given below are six-letter words arranged in circles. They are not jumbled. Find the correct word and write it down. The words can be read clockwise or counter clockwise.

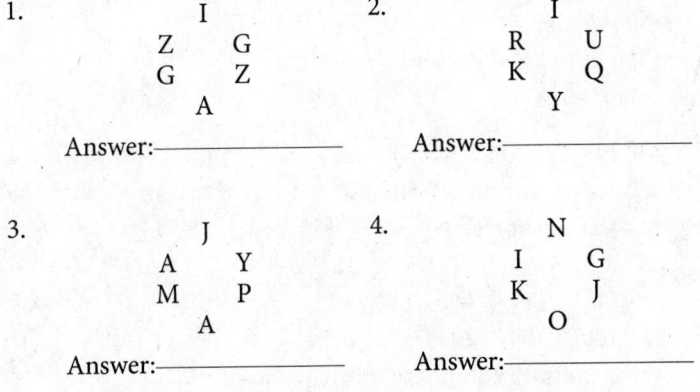

1.
```
        I
    Z       G
    G       Z
        A
```
Answer:—————

2.
```
        I
    R       U
    K       Q
        Y
```
Answer:—————

3.
```
        J
    A       Y
    M       P
        A
```
Answer:—————

4.
```
        N
    I       G
    K       J
        O
```
Answer:—————

5.
```
        B
     I     M
     E     O
        Z
```
Answer:————————

6.
```
           L
        Z     E
        Z     P
           U
```
Answer:————————

7.
```
        K
     C     A
     A     L
        J
```
Answer:————————

8.
```
        U
     J     M
     D     P
        E
```
Answer:————————

9.
```
        E
     L     J
     B     U
        M
```
Answer:————————

10.
```
        Z
     E     Y
     E     B
        R
```
Answer:————————

Exercise 3: Figure It Out!

Focus: Numerical reasoning
Time: 5 minutes
Materials required: Pen/pencil
Level: Beginner's

1. All the mathematical signs (+, −, x, ÷) in the following sums have been omitted. Your task is to insert them so that the answers are correct.
   a) 5 __ 30 __ 23 __ 9 = 118
   b) 11 __ 11 __ 11 = 132
   c) 100 __ 5 __ 20 __ 2 = 117
2. What number completes the sequence?
   a) 68, 64, 32, 28, 14, 10, 5, ____
   b) 2, 3, 5, 7, 11, 13, ____
   c) 3, 6, 18 4, 9, 36 6, ___, 36

3. How many squares are there in the figure below? **Hint:** It's more than 25!

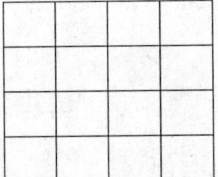

4. Find the missing numbers in the last mathematical matchstick man.

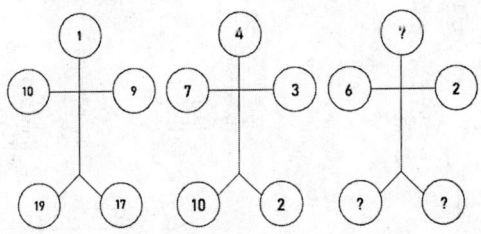

5. Rohit bought a book of tickets for the rides at Fun World. 8 of the tickets were red.

   There were twice as many blue tickets as red tickets.

   He used all 6 of his yellow tickets first.

   How many tickets did Rohit buy altogether?

   Answer:————————————

Exercise 4: Odd Four

Focus: Active Observation
Time: 2 minutes
Level: Beginner's

Find four objects in the following picture that are not repeated. Do not mark off the doubles, rather, try and keep them in your short-term memory.

Exercise 5: Out-Of-The-Box Riddles

Focus: Lateral Thinking
Time: 5 minutes
Level: Beginner's

Lateral thinking problems require you to think 'out of the box'. The clue to solving the riddles may or may not be present in the riddle. Exercise your imagination. Take about one minute per riddle.

1. While travelling, Vinay and Akshay book a room at a hotel. After checking into their room on the eleventh floor, Akshay decides to stay back while Vinay decides to go for a walk. He takes the elevator back down to the ground floor and goes for his walk. He walks for one hour and then returns to the hotel and gets back on the elevator. He presses the button for the eighth floor and grudgingly climbs the remaining floors to their room on the eleventh floor. Why did he do that?

2. Inspector Narayan is called to a holiday resort, to the scene of a suicide. Upon arriving, he finds a tourist dead. She appears to have shot herself. He searches the room, going through the couples' suitcases, wardrobe, shopping bags and travel itinerary. He then arrests her husband for murdering his wife. How does he know that it is murder and not suicide?

3. A perfectly healthy donkey passes the same distance every day, but surprisingly, two of his legs travel 3 kilometres, while his other two legs travel 3.2 kilometres. How is this possible?

4. One day, I was walking down the street and happened by chance to meet my uncle. I had never met him before, nor had I ever seen a photograph of him, but I recognized him immediately. How was this possible?

5. With just one stroke of your pen (one line), turn the number below into a time.
   10 10 10

Exercise of the Day

Today is backwards day. Spend the rest of the day reading things backwards. Try and read billboards and signs, names of shops and street names, etc. from right to left. What does your name sound like backwards? Try and read your text messages and emails from right to left.

Looking ahead: Keep a single playing dice handy. You can take it from any board game that you already have.

Chapter 6

Week 1—Day 4

Today, we will focus on creativity, imagination, short-term memory, working memory and long-term memory.

Exercise 1: Heroes and Villains

Focus: Creativity
Time: 10 minutes
Materials required: Paper/pen, dice
Level: Beginner's

There are three lists of words given below. The first one is a list of objects, the second is a list of heroes and the third is a list of villains. Roll the dice six times. Match the number that shows up on the dice with the corresponding word on the list. Select two words from the objects' list, two words from the heroes' list and two words from the villains' list. Write a short story using all these words. Do not take more than 10 minutes for this exercise. Be as absurd, ridiculous and creative as possible with your story. Do not write down obvious or non-creative answers such as 'Thor threw his hammer at the Riddler' or 'Captain America used his shield against the Green Goblin'.

Note: If you do not have a dice, randomly select two words from each column.

Objects		Heroes		Villains	
1	hammer	1	Hulk	1	Green Goblin

2	shield	2	Thor	2	Penguin
3	spider web	3	Ant Man	3	Joker
4	icicles	4	Wonder Woman	4	Lex Luthor
5	whip	5	Captain America	5	Bane
6	rockets	6	Iron Man	6	Riddler

Scoring: 10 points for completing the exercise on time.

20 points for absurdity and creativity.

0 points for non-creative sentences.

Total score: _____

Exercise 2: Aliens on Earth

Focus: Imagination
Time 10 minutes
Level: Beginner's

Sit down in a quiet place, close your eyes and let your imagination run riot. Imagine that you are an alien who has just landed on Earth. You are from a planet where everything is completely different from Earth—your culture, social norms, food, values, physical appearance, etc., are all different. Keep in mind that many of the things that humans do would probably appear confusing and absolutely ridiculous to you as an alien on this new planet. Have fun with this exercise. Think of all the things that humans do that you, as an alien, find strange or downright crazy and absurd.

Exercise 3: Memorize It!

Focus: Short-term Memory
Time: 6 minutes
Materials required: Paper and pen/pencil
Level: Intermediate

Look at the list below and memorize it, taking not more than 2 minutes. Then, close the book and write all the words down on a piece of paper, taking no more than a minute. Once you are done, look at the hint given below and redo the exercise using the given technique.

sofa	buns	sharpener
bread	stool	rocking chair
stapler	crayons	chicken
eraser	table lamp	paper
chair	bed	couch
milk	chalk	pasta
mangoes	highlighter	envelopes
table	cheese	coffee table
pencil	bean bag	beans
bookshelf	cupcakes	scissors

Hint: Look at the patterns. Can you segregate all the items into three categories of 'furniture', 'stationery' and 'groceries'? Chunk all the items under these categories and you will remember them better. Take two minutes to chunk all the items and another minute to write them down.

Scoring: 10 points for every correct answer.
Your score: ─────────────────────

Exercise 4: Next Please!

Focus: Working Memory
Time: 5 minutes
Materials required: Paper and pen/pencil
Level: Intermediate

Look at the list of numbers below. You can either call them out yourself or ask somebody else to call them out for you. In fact, somebody else calling them out for you would be preferable. Keep a pen and paper handy. Your task is to read the numbers or listen to them and write their *consecutive numbers* down. For example, if the number is 387, you will write the consecutive number down for 3 (4), the consecutive number for 8 (9) and the consecutive number for 7 (8). Therefore, while you read or hear the number as 387, you will write it down as 498. Call out the numbers at an even pace, then close the book and write them down. Ready? Start!

3
56
354
8675
25465
837224
7201383
01738275
482018364
1028362833

Hint: Chunk the larger numbers into groups of smaller numbers. So, a ten-digit number becomes 182-283-8873. Remember it as one hundred and eighty two not as one-eight-two, etc. You can also use the Number Shapes to transform the numbers into images, which will help you remember them better.

Scoring: 1 point for every correct row.
Your score: ————————————————

Exercise 5: Daughters of Memory

Focus: Long-term Memory
Time: 6 minutes
Level: Intermediate
In ancient Greek mythology, Mnemosyne (Nim-aw-sin-ee) was

the goddess of memory. Her daughters were the nine muses who ruled over the arts and sciences and gave artists inspiration.

This exercise is done in two parts. Take 3 minutes for Part 1 and 3 minutes for Part 2.

Part 1: Learn the names of all the nine daughters of Mnemosyne.
Part 2: Learn the names along with the skill of each muse.

The nine muses:

1. Calliope: The muse of epic poetry
2. Clio: The muse of history
3. Erato: The muse of love poetry
4. Euterpe: The muse of music
5. Melpomene: The muse of tragedy
6. Polyhymnia: The muse of sacred poetry
7. Terpsichore: The muse of dance
8. Thalia: The muse of comedy
9. Urania: The muse of astronomy

Hint: Part 1: Use acronyms to learn the names of the muses.
Part 2: Use Pure Links or Story Links to associate each muse with their specific skill.

Scoring: 1 point for every correct answer.

Score for Part 1: —————————————

Score for Part 2: —————————————

Exercise of the Day: Plan and Execute

Plan something and follow through with it. Call or text a few friends and make a plan to meet this weekend. Plan a group activity, perhaps something that you have not done before with this set of friends. The object here is to make a plan and execute it, while making it different from what you and your friends usually do.

Looking ahead: Keep a ball-point pen (preferably with a clicker at the top) that can be opened, ready for tomorrow. You also need five currency coins—three large coins of the same size and two smaller coins of the same size. Perhaps three ten-rupee coins and two five-rupee coins can be used.

Chapter 7

Week 1—Day 5

Today, we will focus on episodic memory, semantic memory, procedural memory, spatial memory and processing speed.

Exercise 1: Having Fun

Focus: Episodic Memory
Time: 10 minutes
Level: Intermediate

If you want to remember past events in its full technicolour details, you must strengthen your episodic memory. Find a quiet place where you can shut your eyes and take yourself back in time. Think of the last time you remember having a lot of fun. Use all your senses to brighten the image and see it more clearly, hear what is being said, feel all the emotions that you were feeling that day. Were you eating something? Were you with friends or family? Once you have the image in your mind, rewind it in your head and start at the very beginning. Remember all the things that you did that day. Try and remember the conversation. What were you laughing about? Who said what? How did that day end? Try and replay that entire day like a movie in your mind, seeing the images clearly.

Exercise 2: The Big Five

Focus: Semantic Memory
Time: 10 minutes

Materials required: Pen/pencil
Level: Intermediate
Name five of the following:

1. Any five coastal cities in India: —————————————

2. Any five presidents of India: —————————————

3. Any five states in North India: —————————————

4. Any five countries that border India: ———————————

5. Any five languages spoken in South India: ——————

6. Any five cities in India that are landlocked (are not near a sea or ocean): —————————————

7. Any five rivers of India: —————————————

8. Any five Indian cricketers: —————————————

9. The names of any five airports in India: ——————————

10. Any five iconic temples in India: —————————————

Exercise 3: Break it Down

Focus: Procedural Memory
Time: 5 minutes
Materials required: A ball-point pen that can be opened
Level: Intermediate

Procedural memory is the kind of memory that tells you how

to do things.

Today, you will focus on how to dismantle and reassemble a simple ball-point pen. First, observe the pen. Does it have a cap? Does it have moveable parts? If you click it on top, what is the mechanism that allows the nib to emerge from the other end? Now, open the pen and remove all the parts. Arrange each part on the table in front of you. Once you have done this, put them all back together again. Does the pen work fine?

Note: While you have just dismantled and reassembled a simple pen, try this with other objects as well. Try to dismantle your alarm clock or any other toy and put it back together again. The more you do this, the more you will understand how seemingly simple things around you work.

Exercise 4: Spatial Puzzles

Focus: Spatial Memory
Time: 10 minutes
Materials required: Paper and pencil, three ₹10 coins and two ₹5 coins
Level: Intermediary

1. In the following puzzle, the aim is to draw lines linking the same shapes. There is only one rule. None of the lines must cross each other.

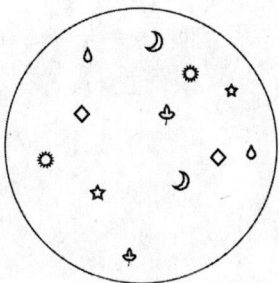

2. Arrange three ₹10 coins and two ₹5 coins (or any three large coins and two smaller coins) alternately as shown in the picture below. You need to change their positions to those shown in the second row in the shortest possible number of moves. Try to do it in five moves or less.

Rules:

- You need to move two coins at a time. One coin needs to be a large coin and the other needs to be a smaller coin. You cannot move one single coin at a time nor can you move two coins of the same size together.
- The two coins that you move must be adjacent coins (coins next to each other).
- The coin on the left must always remain on the left while the coin on the right must always remain on the right while you are moving it.
- Gaps in the chain are allowed in any move except the final move.

Brain challenge: Try manipulating the coins in your mind rather than with real coins.

Starting position:

Final position:

3. Look closely at the ropes below. How many of these loops will form a knot if the rope is pulled taut?

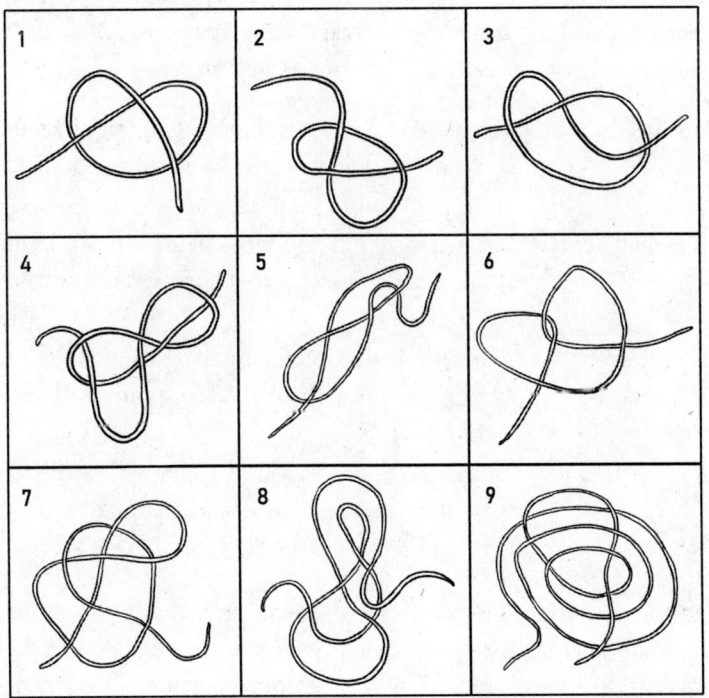

Exercise 5: Slap Slap Tap Tap

Focus: Processing Speed
Time: 7 minutes
Level: Intermediate

Sit at a table with this book flat in front of you. Weigh the pages down so that they don't move while you are doing this exercise. Place both your hands, palms facing downwards on the table and keep both feet firmly on the ground. The exercise below consists of calling out four letters—b, d, p and q. Each letter corresponds to a particular body part. When the letter is called out, you need to tap the corresponding hand or foot. Take a minute or so to learn the letters and their corresponding hand or foot before starting the exercise. The letters are as follows:

p = Right foot.   The letter 'p' has the loop facing right while its stem goes downwards so it corresponds to your right foot.

q = Left foot.   The letter 'q' has the loop facing left while its stem goes downwards so it corresponds to your left foot.

b = Right hand.   The letter 'b' has the loop facing right while its stem goes upwards so it corresponds to your right hand.

d = Left hand.   The letter 'd' has the loop facing left while its stem goes upwards so it corresponds to your left hand.

As you read the letters aloud, tap the appropriate body part at the same time. Do this as fast as possible. Time yourself. Repeat the exercise five times and see if you can beat your previous time.

p	q	d	b	p	q	d	b	p	q
d	q	p	b	q	b	p	d	q	b
b	d	p	q	p	p	d	b	q	q
p	d	b	q	d	b	q	d	b	p
q	p	d	p	b	d	q	d	p	b
q	d	b	b	d	p	d	q	p	d
p	b	q	b	d	d	q	p	b	q

Time 1: ———————

Time 2: ———————

Time 3: ———————

Time 4: ———————

Time 5: ———————

Exercise of the Day: Point it Out!

Time: 15 minutes

We'll continue with the theme of the day with another spatial exercise. You can try this one in the evening or just before going to bed.

Shut your eyes and imagine different objects in the room around you. With your eyes still shut, point to different objects in turn as accurately as you can. Practise this until you can be sure that you've got it right with every single object. Carry on until you can pinpoint at least twenty objects in the room accurately, with your eyes shut.

Recall Sheet for Week 1—Day 4: Daughters of Memory

Remember the nine daughters of memory that you memorized yesterday? Without looking, test your long-term memory, and write all the names of the muses down below with their specific skills.

1. _____

2. _____

3. _____

4. _____

5. _____

6. _____

7. _____

8. _____

9. _____

What is the name of their mother?

_____

Chapter 8

Week 1—Day 6

Today, we will focus on logic, analytical skills, comprehension, language and numerical reasoning.

Exercise 1: Seating Arrangements
Focus: Logic
Time: 5 minutes
Materials required: Paper and pen/pencil
Level: Intermediate

1. Four married couples—Aysha and Sameer, Mansi and Nikhil, Kavery and Hari, and Diya and Praveen (the hosts)—were celebrating Praveen's birthday. Everybody was sitting at a round table in such a way that each lady was seated between two gentlemen, and all the couples were separated. Aysha took her seat between Nikhil and Praveen. Praveen sat to the right of Aysha. Sameer was sitting next to Diya. Who took the seat to the right of Mansi?

Hint: It helps if you draw a round table and place each person at their seats. Start with the person whose position is stated clearly.

2. Six friends—Nisha, Swathi, Ravi, Prakash, Rohan and Vipin—go to the theatre to watch a movie. Unfortunately, they don't get tickets to sit together. They are instead, spread over four rows like so:

    *   Nisha's partner is sitting on her left.

- Prakash's view is blocked by Ravi.
- Ravi's sister is sitting with Vipin in the same seat number as Nisha.
- Rohan is alone in the third row.

Where is everybody sitting?

Hint: It helps to draw the four rows and start with the person whose position is clearly stated.

3. Sitting around a rectangular table are three girls: Diksha, Cauvery and Preethi.
   Sitting with them are three boys: Benny, Aakash and Vinay.
   Two of the girls sat next to each other.
   Aakash sat opposite Benny.
   Vinay sat to Cauvery's left.
   Cauvery did not sit beside Diksha or Preethi.
   Vinay sat opposite Preethi.
   Place each person at their seats at the table below:

Exercise 2: Whodunnit?

Focus: Analytical Skills
Time: 5 minutes
Level: Intermediate

Use the hidden clues in the following puzzles to figure out the answer.

1. On a snowy winter night, a man was resting in front of a fireplace. Suddenly, a snowball smashed through

his window and landed beside him. The man rushed to the window and saw four neighbourhood kids running away. They were brothers named Mathew Anderson, Mark Anderson, Luke Anderson and John Anderson. The next day, a paper note was left on the man's door which read, '?Anderson. He threw the snowball'. The man immediately knew who had thrown the snowball. Who was the culprit, and how did the man know?

2. A Japanese ship was sailing on the open sea. The captain absent-mindedly removed his gold wedding ring and left it on the table in his cabin. When he remembered, he came back for it, but it had gone missing. He suspected three crew members of stealing it and started questioning them on their whereabouts.

    The cook said, 'I was in the kitchen preparing tonight's dinner'.

    The engineer said, 'I was working in the engine room making sure everything was running smoothly'.

    The seaman said, 'I noticed that the flag was upside down, and so, I was on the mast, correcting it'.

    The captain immediately knew who it was. How?

3. A chemist was murdered in his lab. The only evidence was a piece of paper that had the names of chemical substances—nickel, carbon, oxygen, lanthanum and sulphur—written on it. Only four people had come by the lab on the day of the murder—the chemist's wife Sarah, their nephew Nicolas, their friend Mark and another chemist named Jessica. The police immediately knew who the murderer was. Who was it and how did they know?

4. John was murdered on a dreary Sunday afternoon and was found outside his house, buried in the snow. All the suspects were questioned.

    The gardener said, 'I was in the front yard, clearing snow from the bushes when I found him'.

    The maid said, 'I was upstairs, making the beds'.

    John's sister said, 'I was sitting by the fireplace in the living room and reading a book'.

    The cook said, 'I was getting breakfast ready'.

    John's wife said, 'And I was reading and waiting for my breakfast'.

    The police arrested two people. Who are they and why were they arrested?

5. A detective was murdered in his office. Before he died, he circled some numbers on his calendar—7, 10, 11, 8, 9. The suspects were his colleagues Jadon, Jason, Jonas and Jayla. Who was the murderer?

Exercise 3: Narcissus

Focus: Comprehension
Time: 10 minutes
Materials required: Paper and pen/pencil
Level: Intermediate

Read the following story just once and answer the questions that follow.

Narcissus was the son of the river god Cephissus and the nymph Liriope. He was a young man renowned for his astonishing beauty and physique. All those who met him, men and women alike, fell madly in love with him. His parents began to get worried about this and spoke to the prophet Teiresias. The prophet told them that he would grow old only if he 'didn't get to know himself'.

When Narcissus was sixteen years old, he was walking in the woods when the nymph Echo saw him and fell madly in love with him. She began following him through the woods. He soon began to feel that he was not alone, and, turning around suddenly, asked, 'Who's there?' She quickly hid herself and echoed his words, 'Who's there? Who's there? Who's there?' Satisfied that he was still alone, Narcissus continued on his way. However, he soon started suspecting that he had company again and quickly turned around and called out. Echo immediately echoed his words. This continued for a while until Echo finally decided to show herself to him.

She stepped out from behind a tree and tried to give Narcissus a hug. Since it was a sudden and unexpected move, Narcissus stepped away from her and asked her to leave him alone. Echo was heartbroken and spent the rest of her life alone in the forest, fading away gradually until only the sound of her remained faintly in the wind.

When Nemesis, the goddess of revenge heard this story, she decided to punish Narcissus. One day, when Narcissus was walking by a lake, he started feeling thirsty. He leaned over the lake to drink water but was amazed by his reflection instead. He had never seen anybody so beautiful and entrancing, and he was completely bewitched by his own beauty. Since he could never obtain the object of his desire, he lost his will to live, and he died on the riverbank, unable to take his eyes off his reflection. He thus fulfilled the prophet Teiresias' prophecy—because he got to 'know' himself by seeing himself, he never grew old.

According to the legend, Narcissus is still admiring himself in the waters of the Styx in the Underworld. The myth of Narcissus lives on today, in the form of Narcissus flowers that grow on the riverbanks in Europe. The flower is as beautiful as Narcissus was said to have been and blooms in the Spring.

Questions:

1. Who were Narcissus's parents?
2. What was the name of the prophet?
3. What was the name of the nymph who fell in love with Narcissus?
4. What happened to Narcissus by the lake?
5. What could the moral of this story be?
6. Can you see a parallel between Narcissus and the selfie culture in which we live? What do you think may happen to us as a society if we get too obsessed with ourselves (posting numerous selfies on social media, updating our profile pictures all the time, craving 'likes' or 'upvotes' on our pictures, etc.)?

Exercise 4: Idioms

Focus: Language
Time: 10 minutes
Materials required: Paper and pen/pencil
Level: Intermediate

The following are common phrases and idioms. Try to figure them out. For example:

1. crae: mixed race
2. taking meas: taking half measures

Work out the following:

1.

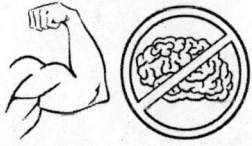

2.　　I'm
　　　Moon

3.

4.　　5.30 just a.m.

5.

6.

7.

8.　　my i i
　　　bag bag

9.

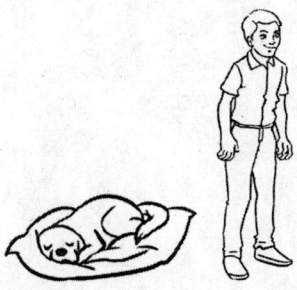

10.

11.

12.   the head clouds

13. |R|E|A|D|I|N|G|

14.

15.

Exercise 5: Figure It Out!

Focus: Numerical Reasoning
Time: 15 minutes
Materials required: Paper and pen/pencil
Level: Intermediate

1. Fill in this magic square so that the columns, rows and diagonals all add up to the number 2001. Two numbers have already been provided.

	1	
2		

2. a) Mexico City is 13 hours behind Singapore, which is seven hours ahead of London. If it is 4:10 a.m. on Tuesday morning in London, what day and time is it in the other two cities?

    b) You leave Madrid at 3:30 p.m. and fly to Los Angeles in 16 hours. Madrid is nine hours ahead of Los Angeles. To what time should you reset your watch?

c) Shalini's trip home from work takes 32 minutes. What is the latest time she can leave work to reach home at a quarter before five?

3. Which number is missing from Triangle B?

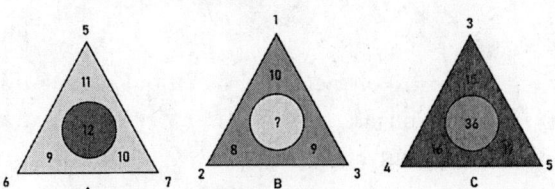

Exercise of the Day: Blind Walk

Today's exercise is spatial in nature. Either blindfold yourself or just close your eyes. Starting at your front door, walk through your house to the furthest wall, without looking. You should not bump into any furniture or walls, or trip over anything.

Think this exercise is too easy? Let's make it slightly harder. Try the same exercise but this time, in addition to having your eyes closed or blindfolded, try walking *backwards* from one end of your house to the other.

Chapter 9

Week 1—Day 7

Today, we will focus on active observation, lateral thinking, creativity, imagination and a word search puzzle to train the left hemisphere of your brain.

Exercise 1: Odd Three

Focus: Active Observation
Time: 5 minutes
Level: Intermediate

This exercise is a two-fold exercise. Look at the images below and find *pairs* of objects. For example, hand and glove, foot and socks, etc. In the entire image, there are three objects that do not have pairs. Find these three objects. Do not mark off the pairs, rather, keep note of them in your mind and remember them.

Objective of this exercise:

1. Find pairs.
2. Find three objects that do not have a pair.

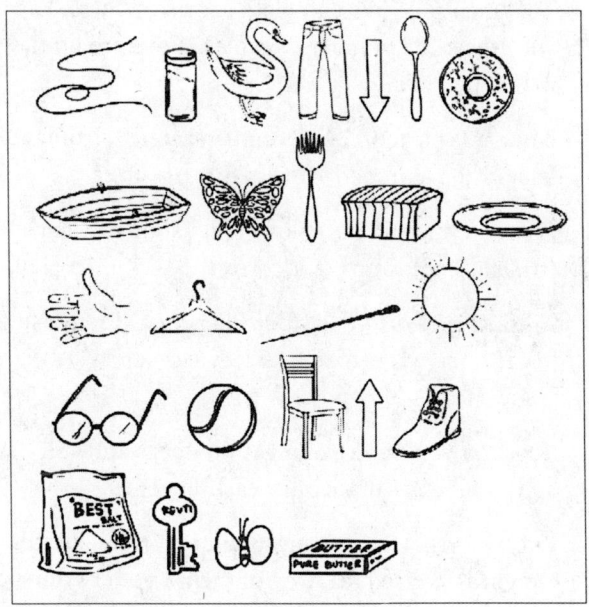

Exercise 2: Out-Of-The-Box Riddles

Focus: Lateral Thinking
Time: 15 minutes
Level: Intermediate

Try and solve the following mysteries as quickly as possible. You need to use your lateral thinking skills, which means that you need to think out of the box to arrive at the solutions to these problems. The clue may or may not be present in the problem.

1. A man stands on one side of a wide river, with his dog on the other bank. The man calls for his dog. Without hesitation, the dog crosses the river; he does not use a bridge or a boat. The dog does not get wet in the process. How is this possible?

2. Two men play five complete games of chess. Each man wins the same number of games. There are no ties. How is this possible?

3. Anna was born on 24 December, yet her birthday always falls in the summer. How is this possible?

4. How can you alter the following equation by a single stroke (straight line) to make it correct? 5 + 5 + 5 = 550.

5. A horse is tied to a 20-foot-long rope. The horse wants to get some water that is 30 feet away and gets the water easily. How is this possible?

6. How can you put 21 oranges in 4 bags and still have an odd number of oranges in each bag?

7. Two women were having dinner at a restaurant. They both ordered iced tea. One of them was very thirsty, and so, she gulped down the iced tea immediately. She had three glasses during the time that it took for the other to have only one. Tragically, the woman who was drinking her iced tea slowly died while the other woman who had drunk three glasses was alive. However, the police found that all the iced teas that they had been served contained poison. How is it possible that the woman who drank more survived?

8. A man walked outside in a heavy rainstorm for twenty minutes without getting a single hair of his head wet. He didn't wear a hat, carry an umbrella or hold anything over his head. His clothes got soaking wet though. How could this happen?

9. How many times can you subtract the number 5 from 20?

10. A basket contains 5 apples. Do you know how to divide them among 5 kids so that each one has an apple and one apple still remains in the basket?

11. A man needs to cross a river. There is a boat that he can take but it can only take one thing at a time. The man has 3 things he must take. A fox, a sheep and cabbage. If he were to take the fox, the sheep would eat the cabbage. But if he were to take the cabbage, the fox would eat the sheep. How would the man take the items across?

12. A man is imprisoned in a dungeon. High up on one of the walls is an unbarred window, but it is too high for him to reach. So the man abandons the hope of escaping through it. He decides to dig his way out instead. However, hours later, he stops as he realises that it would take his entire lifetime to tunnel out. A few days later, an idea comes to his mind, and he begins to dig again. Can you guess what his plan is?

13. As I was going to St. Ives, I met a man with seven wives. Each wife had nine sacks. Each sack had nine cats. Each cat had five kittens. Kittens, cats, sacks and wives, how many were going to St. Ives?

14. A woman was in court for killing her husband. She said she wasn't guilty and that she dearly missed him. In the closing statement, the woman's lawyer stands up and says, 'Her husband was just missing. Everyone look at the doors. He's going to walk through them in about 30 seconds.'

    The entire jury stares at the doors waiting for this woman's husband to walk through the doors.

    The lawyer and the woman stare at the jury.

    The lawyer concludes by saying, 'See! If you were so

sure she killed her husband, you wouldn't be watching that door!'

The jury immediately gave a guilty verdict. Why?

15. A serial killer kidnapped five different people and sat them down each with two pills in their hand and a glass of water. He told them each to take one pill but warned them that one was poisonous and the other was harmless. Whichever pill the victim didn't take, the serial killer would take. Every victim somehow chose the poisonous pill and died. How did the serial killer get them all to take the poisonous pill?

Exercise 3: First and Last Stories

Focus: Creativity
Time: 10 minutes
Level: Intermediate

Make up a story of any length, beginning and ending with the following phrases. Give yourself one minute to think of the story and one minute to narrate it out loud. It must begin and end with the exact phrases listed below. Sometime during the day, if you have more time, try and flesh out the story and make it a full-sized short story. If narrating it isn't your style, take more time and write it down.

1. 'It's not that I passed out, exactly. When you actually pass out, it feels like .... 'I know,' I said, and reached out to hug her.

2. Just so you understand what a huge deal this was, let me explain some things .... I don't know how long I stood there, dumbfounded.

3. I found the box buried deep behind one of the gravestones at the cemetery................. She waited for them to leave. Then she pounced.

4. The traveller woke up alone beside the raging fire ....Something detached itself from the shadows and followed him.

5. He knew he had to leave. If he left now, he could convince himself that his sight had deceived him..................... .... She opened the door. 'Any idea how long you'll be?'

Exercise 4: Earth without Humans

Focus: Imagination
Time: 10 minutes
Level: Intermediate

If human beings ceased to exist on Earth as of this very moment, what changes do you think would take place on the planet? Do you think Earth would begin to heal itself or would it be completely destroyed? What would happen to buildings, vehicles, forests, oceans, etc.? Be as creative and imaginative as you like.

Exercise 5: Word Search

Focus: Left Brain Function
Materials required: Pen/pencil, stopwatch
Level: Intermediate

1. Find the word Mississippi. It appears only once in this entire grid. It may appear forwards, backwards, top to bottom, bottom to top or diagonally, in any direction.
2. Find the number 1.
3. Find the number 5.

Time yourself and do it as fast as possible.

M	S	I	P	P	I	I	S	S	M	I	P	P
I	I	S	M	S	M	M	I	S	S	P	S	S
S	M	S	I	S	I	I	P	M	S	1	P	M
S	M	I	M	I	S	P	S	I	M	P	S	S
I	I	S	S	P	S	P	I	S	S	I	P	P
P	I	S	S	P	I	I	S	M	I	S	S	I
S	S	I	I	I	P	S	S	S	S	P	I	S
I	S	P	S	P	P	P	I	S	S	S	P	P
P	I	P	P	I	S	S	I	S	S	I	M	I
P	I	P	I	P	S	P	P	M	I	S	S	P
I	P	I	P	S	S	M	P	P	I	S	I	S
5	P	S	P	I	I	S	S	I	P	P	I	M
S	I	S	I	S	P	S	M	P	S	M	I	S

Exercise of the Day: Say NO to Social Media!

Since today's exercises were about creativity and imagination, let's try an exercise that may enhance your creativity further— No Social Media Day! This means that you need to abstain from Facebook, Instagram, Twitter, etc. Disable all notifications from all social media sites on your phone or computer so that you will not be tempted to check any of your accounts. While you're at it, try and make it a no-gadget day as well. Use your mobile phone only to make or receive phone calls and nothing else. Identify other activities that you can do without any of your social media acting as distractions. You'll be surprised as to how creative you can be without social media or gadgets! It's only for one day. You can do it!

Chapter 10

Week 2—Day 1

Welcome to the second week of 'Train your Brain'. As you may have noticed, the exercises in Week 1 started at the beginner's level and then moved into the intermediate level. This week, the exercises will start at an advanced level and move into the expert level. Don't let this deter you though. The idea is to challenge your brain, not keep it at the same level. If you are under twenty years of age or over sixty years of age, take an extra minute or two for each exercise this week, but make it a point to complete all exercises.

Exercise 1: Number Punching

Focus: Short-term Memory
Time: 15 seconds per line
Materials required: Paper and pen/pencil
Level: Advanced

Look at the lists of numbers below. Read the first line, close the book and write the number down. Then read the second line, close the book and write the number down. Follow these steps for all the lists. If possible, ask somebody to call out the numbers. Once the person finishes calling out the first line, write it down immediately. Count the numbers that you got right and write your score down next to each line.

Hint: Chunk the numbers or convert them into images using number shapes. You can then use pure links or story links to link longer numbers with each other. For example, if the number is 27167464, using number shapes, you can convert it to duck, candy cane, candle, elephant's trunk, candy cane, sailboat, elephant's trunk and sailboat. Now make up a simple story with all these words in the same order and you will be able to remember the number long enough to write it down. For example, a duck eating a candy cane and holding a candle bumps into an elephant's trunk. She gives the elephant her candy cane and gets onto a sailboat. The elephant also gets on the sailboat. This method might sound too long winded but the more you practise it, the faster you will be able to convert numbers to images.

3812	Your Score: ————
19302	Your Score: ————
018739	Your Score: ————
1293930	Your Score: ————
01739163	Your Score: ————
173902719	Your Score: ————
19283017304	Your Score: ————
183743927302	Your Score: ————
5630273928203	Your Score: ————
18294756392017	Your Score: ————
102394847592745	Your Score: ————
1199388302201933	Your Score: ————
11938273929384782	Your Score: ————
546735186452836452	Your Score: ————

Exercise 2: Word Rows

Focus: Working Memory
Time: 5 minutes
Materials required: Paper and pen/pencil
Level: Advanced

Look at the words below and memorize them row by row. You should know all the words in their correct order in row 1, all the words in their correct order in row 2, etc. Once you are done, cover the grid and write down the words in the blank grid provided below, taking care to follow the order. Take 3 minutes to memorize the words and 2 minutes to write them down.

1	Rainbow	Monday	Kitchen	Boxer	Puppy
2	Mother	Seven	Pizza	Donate	Turtle
3	Forest	Desert	Hammer	Future	Heaven
4	Pirate	Dinner	Supper	Doctor	Hero
5	Violet	Lilac	Yellow	Purple	Magenta

Hint: You can use acronyms to remember the words in their correct order. You can also use a simple story with five sentences, one sentence per line, using all five words. Try to chunk the words into groups of five and tag them to each number. Look for patterns within the groups.

4					
3					
5					
2					
1					

Exercise 3: Prime Ministers of India

Focus: Long-term Memory
Time: 6 minutes
Materials required: Paper and pen/pencil
Level: Advanced

The following exercise is in two parts:

Part 1: Learn the names of the first ten prime ministers of India. Take 2 minutes to learn the names and 1 minute to write them down.
Part 2: Learn the years that they served as prime ministers. Take 2 minutes to learn the years and 1 minute to write them down.

1.	Jawaharlal Nehru:	1947–1964
2.	Gulzarilal Nanda:	1964 (Interim)
3.	Lal Bahadur Shastri:	1964–1966
4.	Gulzarilal Nanda:	1966 (Interim)
5.	Indira Gandhi:	1966–1977
6.	Morarji Desai:	1977–1979
7.	Charan Singh:	1979–1980
8.	Indira Gandhi:	1980–1984
9.	Rajiv Gandhi:	1984–1989
10.	V.P. Singh:	1989–1990

Exercise 4: Down Memory Lane

Focus: Episodic Memory
Time: 10 minutes
Level: Advanced

Find a quiet place where you can shut your eyes and take yourself back in time. If you are currently a student, think of the route that you used to take to primary school. If you are an adult, think of the route that you used to take to high school. See yourself going through your morning routine as a student. Picture all the little details that were involved in getting ready for school, leaving the house and reaching school. What time did you wake up each day? Did your parents drop you or did you cycle to school? Did you take the school bus or public transport? Envision the route and all the shops that you passed and the people that you come across every day. Recollect the names of the streets that you travelled through and the names of the shops that you passed. Try and remember every little thing that you did from the time you woke up till you reached school. See these images clearly in your mind and then slowly bring yourself back to the present.

Exercise 5: Your World

Focus: Semantic Memory
Time: 10 minutes
Level: Advanced

Your general knowledge and knowledge of the world around you are part of your semantic memory. Last week, you took a general knowledge quiz that had three options per question. The options test your power of recognition. Sometimes, even if you do not know the answer, you may be able to deduce it correctly by looking at the options. Today, you will test your ability to recall rather than recognize by relying on your long-term semantic memory to remember the answers without options.

1. How long does a day in the polar regions last?
2. What is an iguanodon?
3. What are trees that lose their leaves in winter called?
4. The shortest war recorded in history lasted for 38 minutes and was fought between which two countries?
5. Who defined democracy as a 'Government of the people, by the people and for the people'?
6. What is another word for 'lexicon'?
7. Who invented the rabies vaccination?
8. Name the world's biggest island.
9. Which country is Prague located in?
10. Which garden is considered to be among the Seven

Wonders of the Ancient World?

11. Name the country where you would find the 'Cresta Run'.
12. Which chess piece can only move diagonally?
13. What is the painting 'La Gioconda' more commonly known as?
14. Which Shakespeare play features Shylock?
15. What is sushi traditionally wrapped in?
16. What is the best type of grain used in brewing beer?
17. Who employed Jeeves in the PG Wodehouse novels?
18. Who wrote 'Cat on a Hot Tin Roof?'
19. Which American President was the first to appear on TV?
20. Mancunium was the Roman name for which English city?
21. Line dancing is associated with which type of music?
22. How would a test match cricketer qualify for the primary club?
23. Following the Vietnam War, what was Saigon renamed as?
24. What does the acronym 'WYSIWYG' stand for?
25. What was the first antibiotic used in medicine?

Exercise of the Day: Left-nostril Breathing

You've had quite a brain work out today! You can end the workout by practising some left-nostril breathing to calm your mind. This exercise can be done any time during the day, but would be more effective just before bedtime, to help you calm down and sleep better.

Sit comfortably. Take your right hand and, with your fingers outstretched, block off your right nostril by putting gentle pressure on it with your right thumb. Be sure to keep the rest of your fingers straight and pointing up towards the sky. With a long, slow, deep breath, gently inhale through your left nostril. Then, just as gently, exhale slowly and completely, again through the left nostril. Relax your entire body as you feel the cooling breath bringing new life into your body. Relax a bit more with each exhalation as you breathe out all your tension and stress. Continue doing this for as long as you like.

Looking ahead: Keep a deck of playing cards ready for tomorrow's exercises.

Chapter 11

Week 2—Day 2

Today we will be focusing on procedural memory, spatial memory, processing speed, logic and analytical skills.

Exercise 1: Card Magic
Focus: Procedural Memory
Time: 20 minutes
Materials required: A deck of playing cards
Level: Intermediate–advanced

Card tricks are always good entertainment, especially when you want to impress your friends and family with your amazing psychic abilities in guessing their card correctly. However, before you begin mystifying your awed audiences, you need to master certain sleight-of-hand moves that are a part of every card trick. As with all skills, this may be difficult at first but will become easier the more you practise. Today, you will learn two simple card tricks but before wowing an audience, you need to learn and practise them.

Trick 1: Count twenty
The trick: Cut a full deck of cards into two piles. Ask a friend to select a card and then place it on the deck. You will then put both piles together and pick the correct card without looking at any of the cards!

Steps:

1. This trick does not require a sleight-of-hand move, but you will need to 'cut' the pack into two by counting out exactly twenty cards without actually showing that you are counting them. This is your 'Pile 2' while the remaining cards are 'Pile 1'.

2. Offer the other half of the pack (Pile 1) to your friend. Ask him to choose a card, memorize it and give it back to you.

3. When you get the card, slip it under Pile 2 so that all twenty cards are on top of it.

4. Now take all twenty-one cards and place them on top of Pile 1.

5. Starting at the top, flip the cards over one by one while counting to twenty in your head. With a flourish, show your friend the twenty-first card and say, 'Here's your card!' He or she is guaranteed to be amazed!

Tips:

- Counting exactly is very important in this trick. Practise counting in your head without moving your lips so that nobody knows that you are counting.

- When you first separate the pack into two piles, it needs to look like you are simply cutting the cards when, in fact, you will be taking exactly twenty cards from the pack. You need to practise this.

- If you are not confident, try setting aside Pile 2 beforehand when nobody is watching.

Trick 2: Upside-down card

The trick: This trick is slightly more difficult than the previous trick and requires some amount of practice. Your friend selects a card, memorizes it and places it back into the deck. After placing the deck behind your back and bringing it out again almost immediately, the selected card has magically reversed itself in the entire pack!

Steps:

1. Prepare the deck of cards by reversing the bottom card so that it is facing upwards when all the other cards are facing downwards. This is the most important step.
2. In front of your friend, take out the deck and fan it out so that all the cards are facing down. Your friend should never notice that the bottom card is facing the wrong way.
3. Ask your friend to select a card. While he is looking at the card, casually turn the deck so that the reversed bottom card is now on top facing down. To spectators, it will still look like all the cards are facing down when in fact it is only the top card that is facing down.
4. Keep the deck together and without spreading it, shove the chosen card anywhere in the deck, facing down. You still have not seen the chosen card. It should look as if the card went into a face-down deck when, in fact, this card and the top card are the only two cards that are facing down.
5. Put the deck behind your back and secretly turn over the top card. Now all the cards except for the chosen card are facing the same direction.
6. Bring out the face-up deck and spread all the cards until you find the only one that is facing the wrong direction. You can slowly turn it over to reveal your friend's chosen card.

Tips:

• Practise this trick until you can perform it smoothly.
• Don't repeat this trick in front of the same friend as you

will need to prepare the deck once more by reversing the bottom card.

- Make sure that your friend does not see that the bottom card is reversed.
- Make sure all your friends are in front of you when you are reversing the top card (formerly bottom card) behind you.

Exercise 2: Spatial Puzzles

Focus: Spatial Memory
Time: 20 minutes
Materials required: Paper and pen/pencil
Level: Advanced

1. What is the smallest number that increases by 12 when it is turned upside down?
2. Cogs 1, 2, 3 and 4 have six, seven, eight and nine teeth respectively. Keeping in mind that the letter 'O' in cog 3 is a perfect circle and that the letter 'y' reads correctly three times every revolution, how many complete revolutions of Cog 1 will result in the word 'TROY' being spelt out perfectly again?

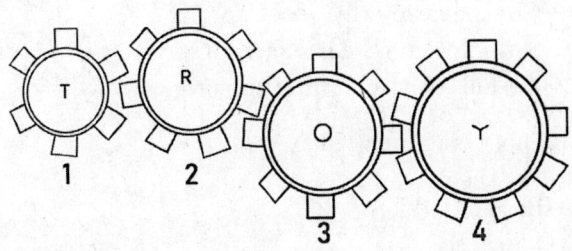

3. Which options below continues the sequence?

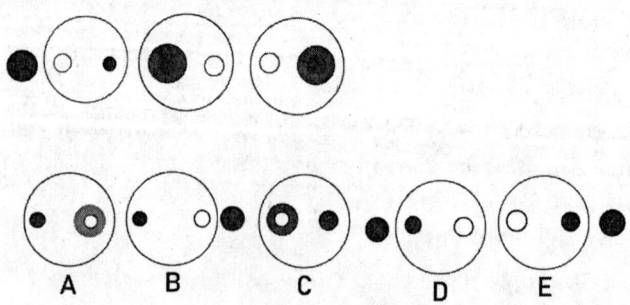

Exercise 3: Odd Unscramble

Focus: Processing Speed
Time: 3 minutes
Material required: Pen/pencil
Level: Advanced

This exercise not only tests your processing speed but your spatial memory and semantic memory as well and is three fold:

1. Unscramble all the letters in all the categories.
2. Find the word that does NOT belong in the category. Circle the word that does not fit.
3. Since this exercise is a speed test, you need to complete the full exercise in three minutes or less.

1. Subjects in high school.
   a) shamt
   b) hgielns
   c) suehos
   d) cesenci
   e) shtyoir

2. Types of trees
   a) cbrih
   b) tltbeo
   c) ybnnaa
   d) enpi
   e) lme

3. Types of furniture
   a) arihc
   b) brdcoapu
   c) ksde
   d) kxottoeb
   e) ssederr

4. Breed of dogs
   a) leoopd
   b) esesmia
   c) xbreo
   d) dnuschdha
   e) rrbaaldo

5. Continents
   a) usaaaitrl
   b) aaattnrcci
   c) giaaler
   d) poruee
   e) caarfi

6. Types of gases
   a) elagnre
   b) gnexoy
   c) lumhei
   d) gneonrti
   e) ydhgerno

7. Types of flowers
   a) lfsiadofd
   b) intrcaano
   c) ssnnehui
   d) oltive
   e) siri

8. Names of languages
   a) keerg
   b) neegni
   c) hssnpai
   d) rnegma
   e) wherbe

9. Types of water bodies
   a) errisv
   b) skale
   c) aess
   d) sametrs
   e) dclsuo

10. House pets
    a) birbat
    b) tahesmr
    c) hheteca
    d) lgsifhod
    e) blvroied

Exercise 4: Out-Of-The-Box Riddles

Focus: Logic
Time: 10 minutes
Material required: Pen/pencil
Level: Advanced

1. Ruby and Michael have six children—Donald, Rebecka, Mia, Faith, Sonali and Layla. Ruby is pregnant with her seventh child, a girl. Ruby and Michael have chosen a name for her that will fit with all the other names. What name have they chosen and why?

   a) Harmony
   b) Love
   c) Tiana
   d) Debora
   e) Melody

2. a) Imagine you are a police officer who is checking to see if there is any underage drinking in a bar. The rule is that if a person is drinking beer, then he must be over 18 years. When you enter the bar, you see four people:

   One is 16
   One is 20
   One is drinking beer
   One is drinking coke

   Which of the drinkers do you need to check out to see if anyone is drinking underage?

   b) Using the same logic that you used above, imagine that a board-game maker has asked you to check that the cards in his game have been printed correctly. The cards are printed with squares and circles on one side and blue and red on the other side. The rule is that if a card has a square on one side, then it is blue on the other side. You are given four of the cards:

   One shows a circle
   One shows a square
   One is blue
   One is red

Which cards do you need to turn over to see if the rule
has been broken?

3. Martin is a strange liar. He lies on six days of the week
but always tells the truth on the seventh day. He made the
following statements on three successive days:
Day 1: 'I lie on Monday and Tuesday.'
Day 2: 'Today, it's Thursday, Saturday, or Sunday.'
Day 3: 'I lie on Wednesday and Friday.'
On which day does Martin tell the truth?

Exercise 5: Whodunnit?

Focus: Analytical Skills
Time: 10 minutes
Materials required: Paper and pen/pencil
Level: Advanced

1. A rather silly car thief stole the car of the chief of police,
without knowing whose car it was. The police immediately
started an investigation. Based on witnesses' accounts, four
suspects that were seen near the car at the time of the crime
were arrested. Because the chief of police took the case very
seriously, he decided to examine the suspects personally. Each
suspect gave three statements during the examinations, which
are listed below:

Suspect A:

1. 'In high school, I was in the same class as suspect C.'
2. 'Suspect B has no driving license.'
3. 'The thief didn't know that it was the car of the chief of police.'

Suspect B:

1. 'Suspect C is the guilty one.'

2. 'Suspect A is not guilty.'
3. 'I never sat behind the wheel of a car.'

Suspect C:

1. 'I never met suspect A until today.'
2. 'Suspect B is innocent.'
3. 'Suspect D is the guilty one.'

Suspect D:

1. 'Suspect C is innocent.'
2. 'I didn't do it.'
3. 'Suspect A is the guilty one.'

With so many contradicting statements, the chief of police lost track. However, he knew that exactly four of the twelve statements were true, but not which ones. Whom did he arrest for stealing his car?

Exercise of the Day: Memory

Since you already have a deck of playing cards today, we'll use them for today's exercise of the day to play a game of 'Memory'. Remove all the jokers (if you have an even number of jokers, keep them) and turn all the 52 remaining cards face down in front of you. You can either arrange them neatly in rows or let them be scattered. Now find matching pairs for each number by turning two random cards over at a time. If they don't match, turn them face down again but remember what cards they were. Move on to the next two cards until you find a pair. Time yourself and see how fast you can find all the pairs.

Since there are four numbers each, you can make it tougher by pairing the red numbers (eg. 3 of hearts and 3 of diamonds) with each other and the black numbers (eg. 3 of clubs and 3 of spades) with each other.

Recall Sheet for Week 2–Day 1: Prime Ministers of India

Remember the first ten prime ministers of India and the years that they served in office? Recall them and write them all below:

1. _____

2. _____

3. _____

4. _____

5. _____

6. _____

7. _____

8. _____

9. _____

10. _____

Chapter 12

Week 2—Day 3

Today, we will focus on comprehension, language, numerical reasoning, active observation and lateral thinking.

Exercise 1: Hercules and the Lion of Nemea

Focus: Comprehension
Time: 15 minutes
Materials required: Paper and pen/pencil
Level: Advanced

Hercules (also known as Herakles) was the son of Zeus and Alcmene. Zeus was a god who was married to the goddess Hera and Alcmene was a mortal woman. Hera was always enraged by her husband's infidelities, and dedicated herself to make Hercules' life as miserable as possible. When she saw how happy Hercules and his wife Megara were, she sent a fit of madness upon Hercules which put him in such a state of rage, that he killed his wife and children. When the madness left him and he saw what he had done, Hercules was filled with remorse and asked Apollo to cleanse him of his sins.

In order to atone for his sins, Apollo asked Hercules to do ten tasks (which later became twelve). To make it worse, Hercules was to serve his cousin, King Eurystheus (You-riss-thee-us) for twelve years while he completed all the tasks. Eurystheus had a reputation for being cunning and mean and was sure to give Hercules a tough time. The good news, however, was that if

Hercules completed all the tasks, Apollo promised to make him a god and he would be immortal.

King Eurystheus had heard of a ferocious lion that was terrorizing a nearby village, and sent Hercules to first kill it and then bring back its skin as his first task. Many heroes had tried and failed to kill the lion and Eurystheus expected Hercules to die in the process.

According to one version of this myth, the Nemean lion took women as hostages to its lair in a cave near Nemea, luring warriors from nearby towns to save the damsel in distress. The lion could shape shift and could assume the form of an injured woman. When the warriors tried rescuing the woman, the lion would change back into its true form and devour them and give their bones to Hades as an offering. King Eurystheus was more than happy to send Hercules to this fate.

Hercules wandered the area until he came to a town named Cleonae. There he met a boy who told him that if Hercules could slay the lion and return alive within thirty days, the whole town would sacrifice a lion to Zeus, but if he did not return within thirty days or died during that period, the boy would sacrifice himself to Zeus. Another version of the same story claims that Hercules met Molorchos, a shepherd who had lost his son to the lion. Molorchos told him that if he returned alive within thirty days, he would sacrifice a ram to Zeus, but if he died, the ram would be sacrificed to Hercules as a mourning offering.

Unknown to Hercules, the lion's golden fur was impenetrable by arrows. Hercules found this out the hard way. When he finally found the lion and shot it with his arrows, he found to his amazement and horror that the arrows just bounced off the lion's fur harmlessly.

Hercules then had to device a new plan. After pursuing the lion, he cornered him inside a cave that had two entrances. Having blocked one entrance, he hunted down the lion through the other. In the dark and confined cave, Hercules stunned the beast with his club, and, using his immense strength, strangled it to death with his bare hands. During the fight, the lion bit off one of his fingers. Some stories suggest that he shot arrows at it, eventually shooting it in its mouth, where its magic fur could not protect it.

Since his task was to bring back the skin of the lion, Hercules tried to skin it using his knife but he failed. Even in death, the fur was still as impenetrable as it had been when the lion was alive. He then tried sharpening the knife with a stone and even tried with the stone itself. Finally, Athena, noticing the hero's plight, advised Hercules to use one of the lion's own claws to skin the pelt.

When he returned on the thirtieth day carrying the carcass of the lion on his shoulders, King Eurystheus was amazed and terrified of what Hercules might do to him. He forbade Hercules from entering the city ever again. From that point onwards, he would send Hercules his tasks through a messenger but never personally. Eurystheus even had a large bronze jar made for himself in which to hide from Hercules if need be. Eurystheus then warned him that the tasks would become increasingly difficult and true to his word, he kept giving Hercules seemingly impossible tasks.

Some myths suggest that Hercules's armour from that point on, was made from the hide of the lion that he had so valiantly slayed.

Answer the following questions:

1. What was the punishment that Apollo gave Hercules and why? What would be the reward?
2. What ruse did the lion use to lure brave warriors into his lair?

3. What was so special about the lion?

4. What are the two different versions of the story when Hercules entered the town of Cleonae?

5. What are the two different versions of the story behind how Hercules finally killed the lion?

6. How did King Eurystheus react when Hercules got back from his quest?

7. In your own words, what do you think the moral of this story is?

8. In your opinion, do you think completing all twelve tasks can purge Hercules of the sin of killing his family? Explain.

Exercise 2: Word Ladders

Focus: Language
Time: 10 minutes
Materials required: Paper and pen/pencil
Level: Advanced

Lewis Carrol, the author of *Alice in Wonderland* created this puzzle in 1878. Each puzzle consists of two words. Your task is to find a sequence of words (a word ladder) starting with one of the given words and ending with the other given word in such a way that you change only one letter at a time to create a new rung on the ladder.

Rules: The words on the rungs have to be real words. Only one letter can be changed per word. The number of letters per word remains constant at all times (four-letter words will have word ladders containing four-letter words, five-letter words will have word ladders containing five letters, etc.). While your ladders can be of any length, try and complete it within the spaces given. Here are two examples to help you get started:

E.g. 1: Turn CAT into DOG
    CAT
    COT (A to O)
    COG (T to G)
    DOG (C to D)

E.g. 2: Turn GOAT to RAFT
    GOAT
    GOAD (T to D)
    GOLD (A to L)
    GILD (O to I)
    GILT (D to T)
    GIFT (L to F)
    RIFT (G to R)
    RAFT (I to A)

1. Turn MOM into DAD
    MOM
    _____
    _____
    _____
    _____
    DAD

2. Turn FALL to COLD
    FALL
    _____
    _____
    _____
    COLD

3. Take the PIG to his STY
    PIG
    _____
    _____
    _____
    _____
    STY

4. Change DRY to WET
    DRY
    _____
    _____
    _____
    WET

5. Make BREAD from WHEAT
    WHEAT
    _____
    _____
    _____
    _____
    _____
    BREAD

6. COMB your HAIR
    COMB
    _____
    _____
    _____
    _____
    HAIR

7. Turn PINK into BLUE

PINK

_____

_____

_____

_____

BLUE

8. Turn WHITE into
   BLACK

WHITE

_____

_____

_____

_____

_____

BLACK

9. Make COLD, WARM

COLD

_____

_____

_____

WARM

10. Change HATE to LOVE

HATE

_____

_____

_____

LOVE

Exercise 3: Figure It Out!

Focus: Numerical Reasoning
Time: 20 minutes
Materials required: Pen/pencil
Level: Advanced

1. In the following diagram, all the supplied weights (1 gram, 2 grams, 3 grams, 4 grams, 6 grams, 7 grams and 8 grams) need to be placed in the pans—one weight per pan—to balance out the scales perfectly. The weight of the rod and pans may be ignored and the stripes on each rod are exactly the same length. Only the weights are taken into consideration. The numbers on the weights correspond to their respective weightage. Try and complete this puzzle in ten minutes.

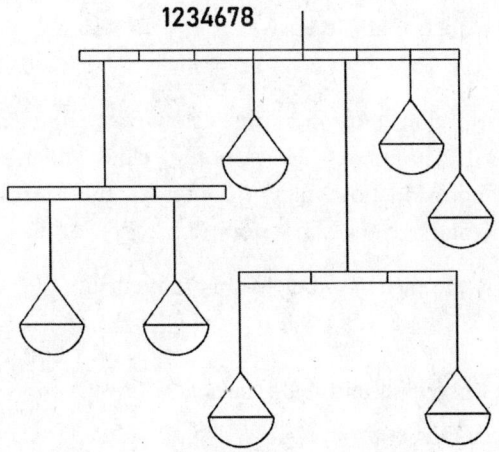

1234678

2. The numbers 1 to 16 must be placed on the square depicted below, in such a way that the sum of each row, column and diagonal amounts to 34. How should the numbers be arranged in the square?

Hint: The sum of each of the four quadrants, the sum of the middle four numbers, the sum of the four corners, the sum of the corners of the two squares formed by the numbers on the sides, and the sum of the numbers on the opposite sides are 34.

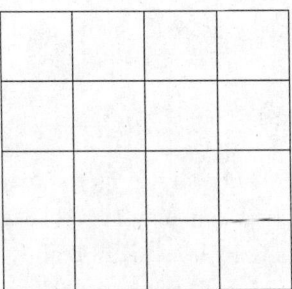

3. Correct the equation shown below by moving just one digit or sign, such that the answer is equal to 1.

$$26 - 63 = 1$$

4. An alarm clock runs 4 minutes slow every hour. It was set right 3 1/2 hours ago. Now another clock which is correct shows noon. In how many minutes, to the nearest minute will the alarm clock show noon?

5. What is the next number in this sequence?

2 9 3 1 8 4 3 6 5 7 _____

Exercise 4: Observing with Five Senses

Focus: Active Observation
Time: 20 minutes
Level: Advanced

As mentioned earlier, observation is perhaps the most important function when it comes to memory. All the inputs in your brain come from your senses. If you don't actively observe something in your environment, you may hear but not listen, touch but not feel, eat but not taste, look but not see and breathe but not smell. You can't remember something that you never knew in the first place. The following exercise trains your powers of observation by training not just your sight, but your other senses of smell, taste, touch and hearing as well. Spend about five minutes with each sense.

Vision

Since your visual memory is so strong, you may often overestimate just how accurate it is. You may start believing that what you imagine in your memory is actually reality. This is not always the case, even with things that we see all the time.

Try to visualize something that you see every day, such as your home, your school or your office. See it clearly in your mind and then try to draw it as accurately as possible. Don't worry too much about your drawing skills—you can represent people as stick figures and buildings as simple line drawings if you want—the aim is to see if you remember details of things rather than testing your artistic skills. You can even label things, if you don't want to draw a complete diagram—as long as you remember what goes where.

Once you finish your drawing, check how accurate you were, against the real thing. You will be surprised as to your accuracy or the lack of it. Did you miss out on any details? Did you add something that's not there in real life? Did you get any of the details wrong?

Sound

There is a difference between hearing and listening. What separates the two is active observation and concentration. If you live or work in a noisy environment, you hear (and ignore) a whole range of sounds. The aim of this exercise is to help you be more aware of everything that you hear and listen to.

Sit on a chair and simply listen to all the sounds around you. What sounds have you heard now that you were not aware of just a few seconds ago? Now move to a different location and try the same exercise there.

Touch

Since we pay more attention to what we see, we pay less attention to our other senses. Collect various coins of different denominations and put them all together in your pocket or your wallet or purse. Now put your hand in and try to identify them by touch alone. Pull each coin out to verify your guess and then put it back in again.

If this was easy, try the same exercise, but this time, include currency coins of different denominations from other countries as well. Think about what criteria you would use to distinguish each coin from the other and a foreign currency coin from yours.

Now see if you can identify the sides of each coin—heads or tails? Try and remember the picture on the 'heads' side of the coin.

Once you improve in this game, you can move to the next level. Get a large bag of small potatoes. Take out six potatoes of different sizes and arrange them randomly in a row. Now, with your eyes firmly on the first potato in the row, put your hand back into the bag and try to pick out a potato of the exact size, by its feel alone. No peeking into the bag! When you find another potato of the same size, pull it out and, without looking at it, arrange it on the table behind you. Repeat this with all the other potatoes in the row in front of you. When you have what you think is a match for all six potatoes, compare the potatoes that you pulled out of the bag with the original six and see how you did.

Once this game gets easier for you, move on to the next difficulty level—identifying fruits or vegetables such as cherries, grapes, etc., that have much more similar sizes.

Taste and Scent

Your tongue can make broad distinctions between five different tastes—sweet, sour, salty, bitter and savoury—while your nose can distinguish approximately 10,000 different aromas! It is for this reason that your nose holds the most scope for training.

For the rest of the day, every time you eat or drink something, spend a minute or two inhaling the aroma, and trying to pick out all the different aromas that make up its identity. Even if you are simply drinking a glass of water, carefully sniff the glass and consider the texture and flavour of the water (there might be a difference between bottled water and regular water). When you eat your next meal, try and guess the ingredients simply by taste. You can close your eyes while you are chewing, to help you concentrate better on the taste.

Exercise 5: Riddles

Focus: Lateral Thinking
Time: 5 minutes
Level: Advanced

Here are a few tricky riddles. Pay special attention to the language used in some of these as there could be hidden clues in them. Try and answer them all in under five minutes. Keep in mind that the focus is on lateral thinking so you will need to think out of the box.

1. Tied up we wander all day
   At night we are let loose
   And lie still with our tongues hanging out.

2. Name an eight letter word that has 'kst' in the middle, in the beginning and at the end.

3. There was a man who was born before his father, killed his mother and married his sister. Yet, there was nothing wrong with what he had done. Why?

4. Though you can walk on water with its power,
   Try to keep it; it will vanish in an hour.

5. Though I am the third,
   I am called the second.
   Though I am not old,
   I do not sound new.

6. It's always 1 to 6,
   It's always 15 to 20,
   It's always 5,

But it's never 21,
Unless it's flying.

7. It's shorter than the rest, but when you're happy, you raise it up like it's the best. What is it?

8. What flies when it is born, lies when it is alive and runs when it is dead?

9. We hurt without moving,
We poison without touching.
We bear the truth and the lies.
We are not to be judged by our size.

10. Two camels were facing in opposite directions. One was facing due east and the other was facing due west. Since they were in a desert at night, there was no reflection or a shadow. How would they manage to see each other without walking around, turning around or moving their heads?

Exercise of the Day: Memorizing Lyrics

Time: 15 minutes

Today's exercise is to sharpen and train your auditory memory. This exercise will be even more enjoyable if you like listening to music. Your task is to listen to one new song today, and try and memorize the lyrics as well as the tune. You can listen to it any number of times within fifteen minutes. At the end of fifteen minutes, try and sing it yourself and see if you remember the tune and the lyrics.

Chapter 13

Week 2—Day 4

Today, we will focus on creativity, imagination, short-term memory, working memory and long-term memory.

Exercise 1: Funny Limericks

Focus: Creativity
Time: Ten minutes
Material required: Pen/ pencil
Level: Advanced

A limerick is a poem that is usually funny, obnoxious, rude and sometimes crude. It has just five lines where the first and second lines rhyme, the third and fourth lines rhyme and the fifth line rhymes with the first and second line. Essentially, the rhyming scheme goes—AABBA. For example, the following is a limerick about a man from Darjeeling (keep in mind that limericks are meant to be funny and crude).

There once was a man from Darjeeling,	(A)
Who got on a bus bound for Ealing.	(A)
It said at the door,	(B)
'Don't spit on the floor'	(B)
So he carefully spat on the ceiling.	(A)

Here's another example of a limerick. This one is a rather sad limerick about a silly lady named Jane.

There once was a lady named Jane,	(A)
Who had sorrows she could not restrain.	(A)
She sobbed and she sighed,	(B)
At each window she cried,	(B)
As she thought of its permanent pane.	(A)

Your task for today is to use the first lines of the following exercise and make up your own limericks. They can be as fun, obnoxious or as naughty as you please. Don't take more than ten minutes for this exercise.

1. There once was an old man from Mars,

   _____

   _____

   _____

   _____

2. There once was a dog that could talk,

   _____

   _____

   _____

   _____

3. There once was a fly and a bee,

   _____

   _____

   _____

   _____

4. There once was a man from Australia,

   _____

   _____

   _____

   _____

5. There once was a young girl of three,

   _____

_____

_____

_____

Exercise 2: Twisted Associations

Focus: Imagination
Time: 5 minutes
Level: Advanced

Look at the following list of words and see how you would either *associate* each word to an ordinary RUBBER BAND or find a novel way of *using* a rubber band with the given word. Try and find as many uses for a rubber band as possible keeping the given words in mind. Avoid obvious answers such as 'A rubber band can be used to tie your hair'. Be as creative and imaginative as possible. There are no wrong answers as long as your uses for the rubber band are plausible and can be explained.

For example, rubber band + toothpick = A rubber band can be stretched over a toothpick to flick pellets at people. Or, a rubber band can be used to keep tooth picks in place while making miniature sculptures.

Hint: Use Pure Links or Story Links described in Chapter 2 for this exercise.

Rubber band: Water bottle ——————————————

Mobile phone ——————————————

Notebook ——————————————

Compact Disk (CD)——————————————

Handbag——————————————

Coffee powder——————————————

Classmate——————————————

Bicycle——————————————

Dart board————————————————————
Steering wheel————————————————
Newspaper—————————————————————
Earphones——————————————————————
Toothbrush——————————————————————
Shoe————————————————————————————
Shaving cream————————————————

Scoring: 10 points for every association and use.

10 points for every creative answer.

Minus 5 for every non-creative answer.

Exercise 3: Sonnet Memory

Focus: Short-term memory
Time: 10 minutes
Materials required: Paper and pen/pencil
Level: Expert

Memorize the sonnet below in not more than ten minutes, then close this book and write it down. Take about a minute to try and understand the poem and also what the poet William Shakespeare is trying to convey before you begin to memorize it.

Sonnet 116: *Let Me Not to the Marriage of True Minds* – William Shakespeare

Let me not to the marriage of true minds
Admit impediments. Love is not love
Which alters when it alteration finds,
Or bends with the remover to remove.
O no! it is an ever-fixed mark
That looks on tempests and is never shaken;
It is the star to every wand'ring bark,
Whose worth's unknown, although his height be taken.

Love's not Time's fool, though rosy lips and cheeks
Within his bending sickle's compass come;
Love alters not with his brief hours and weeks,
But bears it out even to the edge of doom.
If this be error and upon me prov'd,
I never writ, nor no man ever lov'd.

Exercise 4: Months and Their Gemstones

Focus: Working Memory
Time: 10 minutes
Material required: Pen/pencil
Level: Expert

The following is a list of all the months with their associated gem
stones and flowers. Learn the entire list, taking not more than 7
minutes, then turn the page and write them down in the recall
sheet provided. Take about 3 minutes to write everything down.
Do not take more than ten minutes for this entire exercise.

Months	Gem Stone	Flower
January	Garnet	Carnation
February	Amethyst	Primrose, Violet
March	Aquamarine, Bloodstone	Jonquil, Violet
April	Diamond	Daisy, Sweet pea
May	Emerald	Hawthorn, Lily of the Valley
June	Alexandrite, Pearl	Honeysuckle, Rose
July	Ruby	Larkspur, Water Lily
August	Peridot, Spinel	Gladiolus, Poppy
September	Sapphire	Aster, Morning Glory
October	Opal, Tourmaline	Calendula, cosmos
November	Citrine, Topaz	Chrysanthemum
December	Turquoise, Zircon, Tanzanite	Holly, Narcissus, Poinsettia

Recall Sheet: Fill in the gem stones and flowers for the following months.

Months	Gem Stone	Flower
November		
August		
December		
January		
September		
April		
March		
July		
October		
June		
May		
February		

Scoring: 10 points for every correct answer with both gem stones and flowers.

5 points if only gem stone or flower is correct

Your score: ─────────────────

Exercise 5: Professionals and Their Professions

Focus: Long-term Memory
Time: 10 minutes
Materials required: Paper and pen/pencil
Level: Expert

Memorize the following professions along with the description of the type of work that each profession entails. Once you are done, close this book and write everything down on a separate sheet of paper. You need to be able to remember all the professionals and their job descriptions in the correct order from beginning to end. Take seven minutes to memorize the entire list and three minutes to write it down.

Hint: Use the Pure Link or the Story Links method to associate the professional with their work. Use Pure Links or Acronyms method to remember all the professionals in the correct order. Use keywords in each description rather than the entire phrase.

	Profession	Description
1.	Periodontist	A specialist of the gums and other structures around the teeth.
2.	Optometrist	A person skilled in testing for defects of vision in order to prescribe corrective glasses.
3.	Chiropractor	A person who uses spinal adjustments and manipulation to treat certain health concerns such as lower back pain or even headache or high blood pressure.
4.	Podiatrist	A person qualified to diagnose and treat foot disorders.
5.	Anthropologist	A specialist of origins and social relationships of human beings.
6.	Entomologist	A person who studies or is an expert in the branch of zoology dealing with insects.
7.	Endodontist	A dentist specializing in diseases of the dental pulp and nerve.
8.	Psychoanalyst	A person trained to practise a certain set of techniques that explore underlying motives and a method of treating various mental disorders based on the theories of Sigmund Freud.
9.	Taxidermist	A person who prepares and preserves the skin of animals and can stuff and preserve them in life-like form.
10.	Orthopaedist	A specialist in correcting deformities of the skeletal system.

11.	Psychiatrist	A physician who practices diagnosis and treatment of mental disorders.
12.	Obstetrician	A specialist in childbirth and care of the mother.
13.	Dermatologist	A doctor who specializes in treating diseases of the skin.
14.	Ophthalmologist	A doctor who specializes in treatment of the eye and its diseases.
15.	Neurologist	Specialist in the nervous system and the disorders affecting it.

Exercise of the Day: Bon Voyage!

Today has been a tough brain workout. Sit back and relax and think of your next holiday destination. Which city or country would you like to visit? Plan a trip. Look it up. If it is not possible to actually travel, planning itself can be fun. Read up about places that you would like to visit. Talk to friends who have already visited these places and try and get more information from them. Try and contact someone local to see what kind of weather you could expect, what kind of clothes to pack, etc. This will improve your semantic memory, working memory, procedural memory, spatial memory, creativity, imagination and social skills. Trying to make a budget for your travel will improve your numerical reasoning.

Looking ahead: For tomorrow, you will need origami paper or two coloured square sheets of paper.

Chapter 14

Week 2—Day 5

Today, we will focus on episodic memory, semantic memory, procedural memory, spatial memory and processing speed.

Exercise 1: Detailed Recall

Focus: Episodic Memory
Time: 15 minutes
Level: Advanced–expert

The following exercise is two-fold.

1. Answer the questions below without checking the items in real life. This also checks your semantic memory and observation skills.
2. After answering the questions, try and remember every single detail of the act of buying the object in question or the story of how you got it.

For example, the question may be, 'What was the name of your first pet?' Part one of this exercise requires you to answer the question while in part two, you need to think back to the day that you got your first pet. Did your parents buy it for you? Did they surprise you with it? Did you go to the pet store and select it? How were you feeling that day? Were you excited? A bit scared? Nervous? What was your reaction when your pet came home that day? What was the first thing that the pet did at home? Try and think of and remember all the details surrounding the arrival of your first pet.

If the question is 'What brand is your refrigerator?' you will need to answer the question and remember every detail about how you got the refrigerator or the events that led up to its purchase and delivery. Try and remember and recall all the details as clearly as possible. It is not enough just to remember where you bought it—you need to recall all the other information related to it.

1. What is the colour of your current toothbrush?
2. What brand are your slippers?
3. When you turn on your TV, is there a logo that flashes on the screen or a sound that it initially makes?
4. What is the name of the closest shop to your house?
5. Where are your vehicle keys or house keys at this very moment?
6. Without looking up, what colour is your fan and how many blades does it have?
7. When was the last time that you had a haircut?
8. When was the last time that you went out for dinner with your family or friends? Where did you go?
9. How many apps do you have on the home screen of your phone? What is your home screen wallpaper?
10. When was the last time you went shopping? What were the names of the shops that you visited?

Exercise 2: Big Ten

Focus: Semantic Memory
Time: 4 minutes
Level: Expert

Name *ten or more* of the following. The more you name, the more points you get. For example, if the question is 'types of dogs,' you need to name ten or more different breeds such as

German Shepherd, Bulldog, Poodle, Beagle, Golden Retriever, Pug, Rottweiler, Siberian Husky, Boxer, Great Dane, Dachshund, Pit Bull, Doberman, Shih Tzu, etc.

This is a memory test that tests your long-term semantic memory as well as your processing speed, so try and complete the exercise as quickly as possible, taking about 20 seconds or less per item. Ready? Go!

1. Countries in South America
2. Mammals
3. Currencies from different countries
4. Types of fish
5. Clothing retail shops
6. Seas and oceans
7. Current pop stars (any language)
8. Bollywood actresses
9. Car manufacturers
10. Computer and electronics brands

Exercise 3: Origami Art

Focus: Procedural Memory
Time: 10 minutes
Materials required: Two origami papers or two square sheets of paper, preferably coloured
Level: Expert

Today's exercise is to learn to make two origami figures. The first figure is a fox and is relatively easy to make. The second figure is a butterfly, which will require concentration and skill. Once you learn how to make both figures, practise them until you can do it in less than 2 minutes without looking at the instructions.

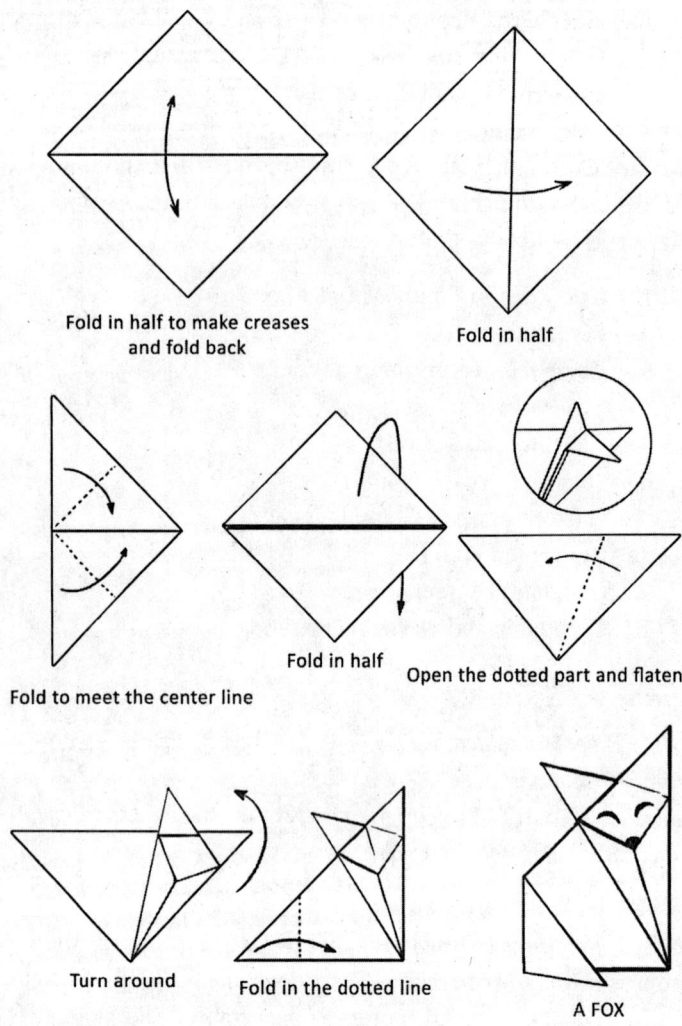

Fold in half to make creases
and fold back

Fold in half

Fold to meet the center line

Fold in half

Open the dotted part and flaten

Turn around

Fold in the dotted line

A FOX

Figure 1: Fox

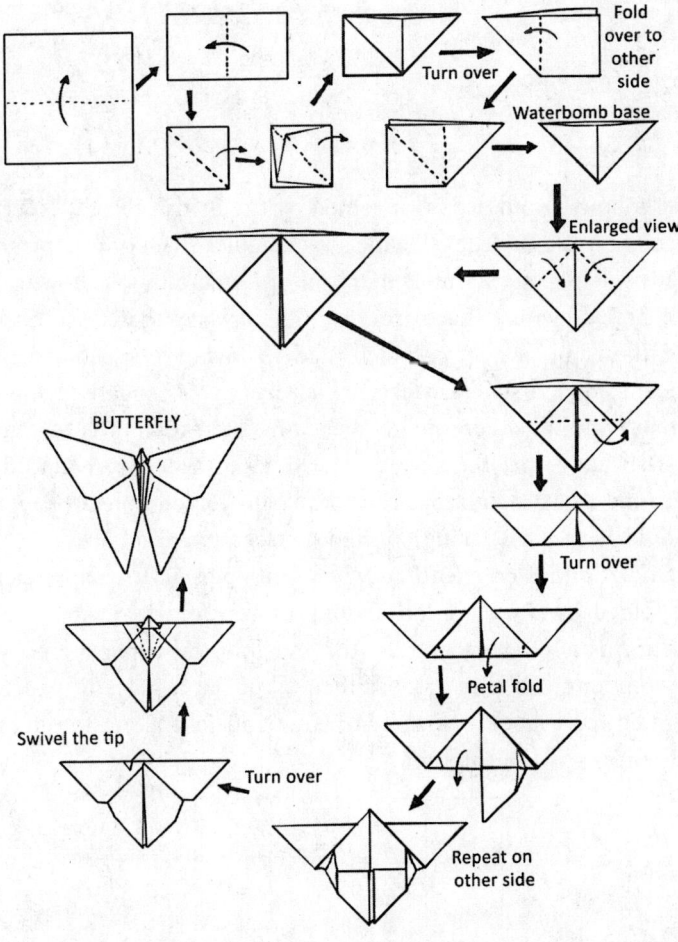

Figure 2: Butterfly

Exercise 4: Spatial Puzzles

Focus: Spatial Memory
Time: 15 minutes
Material required: A sheet of paper
Level: Expert

The following puzzle was invented by the British puzzle expert Henry Ernest Dudeney. Divide a rectangular sheet of paper into eight squares and number them on one side only, as shown in the first drawing. There are 40 different ways that this paper (think of how a map is folded) can be folded along the ruled lines to form a square packet which has the '1' square face-up on top and all other squares beneath. The problem is to fold this sheet so that the squares are in serial order from 1 to 8, with the 1 face-up on top. The completely folded sheet of paper should have the 1 facing out and consecutive numbers of 2, 3, 4, 5, 6, 7 and 8 on each fold when you open it. The paper can be folded in any direction as long as you fold it on the line. Since this is a spatial puzzle, try and fold the paper mentally in your mind. If this is too difficult, cut out a piece of paper, segment and label it as shown below and fold along the lines till you reach the solution.

1	8	7	4
2	3	6	5

When you succeed in doing the above puzzle, try the more difficult level of the same puzzle with another sheet of paper segmented and labelled as follows:

1	8	2	7
4	5	3	6

2. The five pieces below need to be put together to form a square. How can you do this?

Hint: Take a photocopy of this page or trace the image, cut out the pieces and see how to fit them all together. It's not as simple as it looks.

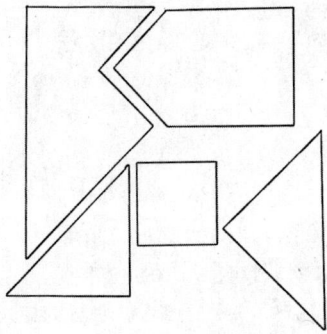

Exercise 5: A+ Word Search

Focus: Processing speed
Time: 20 minutes
Material required: Pen/pencil
Level: Expert

Find and circle the following words in the word search puzzle below. All words begin with the letter A. Most of the words are strange words that you may not have heard before. You need to keep the spellings in mind while looking for them. The words can be found horizontally, vertically or diagonally, in any direction (back to front or bottom to top). Since this is a puzzle that tests your processing speed, try to solve it in twenty minutes or less. Time yourself.

1. AVAILABILITY	19. ARET	37. ACCLOY
2. ABDOMINOUS	20. ARGOSY	38. ACCENSOR
3. ABARTICULAR	21. AVERRUNCATOR	39. AROMA
4. ABASEMENT	22. AVICIDE	40. ACRONYM
5. ABATJOUR	23. ARET	41. AHULL
6. ACERVULINE	24. AMRITA	42. AGLET
7. ACHROMATOPSIA	25. AZIMUTH	43. AGRIZE
8. ACKAMARACKUS	26. AVIONICS	44. ALATE
9. AGORAPHOBIA	27. ARRHIZAL	45. AGGRY
10. ACROBATICALLY	28. AVUNCULAR	46. AILED
11. ACRITOCHROMACY	29. ARGOL	47. AHIMSA
12. ACTINOGRAPH	30. ASEITY	48. AYE-AYE
13. APPARITOR	31. ASCHAM	49. ACER
14. ARCHIDIDASCALIAN	32. ARRONDI	50. ACTING
15. ARCHITECURALIZATION	33. ASSERT	51. AVAILS
16. ARGENTIFEROUS	34. ACATAMATHESIA	52. ANT
17. ARGIL	35. ABY	53. ARK
18. AREOPAGITIC	36. ACCOLADE	54. ACHOR
		55. AIGER

Scoring: 20 minutes or less—Excellent processing speed
   Between 20 and 25 minutes—Very good processing speed
   Between 25 minutes and 30 minutes—Good processing speed
   Above 30 minutes—Average processing speed but can be improved by continuing to work out speed exercises.

Bonus: As a matter of interest, either look up the meaning of these words in a dictionary or Google them.

```
        A C E R V U L I N E A Y B A
        A C A T A M A T H E S I A A D G
      A A R G E N T I F E R O U S V A P A
    A C C O L A D E A C C E N S O R Z V A E
    A E I B A C R O N Y M A E A O A I G E R
    R R T A C R I T O C H R O M A C Y A A A
    C A I T T Y E G N I T C A A I A A B V B
    H R G I I R B T A       A A D S H Z A E D
    I C A C N G C N             E A L U I S R O
    T H P A O G T               A I L M E R M
    E I O L G A                 A L U M U I
    C D E L R C A M A H C S A B V A T E N N
    U I R Y A K A S C I N O I V A A H N C O
    R D A P P A R I T O R L R O H C A T A U
    A A Y A H M A P O A I A S M I H A A T S
    L S S R W A B A R T I C U L A R O A O I
    I C O G A R A A Y E A Y E A A O A A R D
    Z A G O R A P H O B I A P Q V M R S Q N
    A L R L Q C A B A T J O U R U A R E T O
    T I A A R K                 N T H I A R
    I A R E T U                 C O I T T R
    O N Q E Z S                 U P Z Y P A
    N A L A T E                 L S A L C D
    A G R I Z E                 A I L E D A
    A C C L O Y                 R A R G I L
```

Exercise of the Day: Bathroom Space

This activity sharpens your spatial memory and helps you fine-tune it. Find a quiet place at home, sit comfortably and close your eyes.

1. Entirely in your imagination, try moving around your bathroom and brushing your teeth in as much detail as possible. Picture your movements inside the bathroom, where exactly your toothpaste and toothbrush are located, where your bathroom sink is and where the tap is.
2. Once you've got this picture as accurately as possible in your mind, try acting it out where you are. Try it again and remember it in as much detail as you can.
3. Now, with this picture clearly in your mind, go to the bathroom, shut your eyes and try enacting the scene again. Touch the objects whenever appropriate to see how accurate your picture was. Be aware of what you remembered wrong and make adjustments in the picture in your mind.
4. Once you get the hang of this exercise, try it with another everyday task such as getting dressed or setting the table.

Chapter 15

Week 2—Day 6

Today, we will focus on logic, analytical skills, comprehension, language and numerical reasoning skills. Today's exercises will take about 70 minutes in total since they are expert level exercises. Don't do them all at once; try and spread them out through the day, taking a break between each exercise.

Exercise 1: Just Deduce It!

Focus: Logic
Time: 15 minutes
Level: Expert

1. Mr Dutch, Mr English, Mr Painter and Mr Writer are all teachers at the same secondary school. Each teacher teaches two different subjects. Furthermore:

   Three teachers teach the Dutch language;
   There is only one maths teacher;
   There are two teachers for chemistry;
   Two teachers, Simon and Mr English, teach history;
   Peter does not teach the Dutch language;
   Steven is the chemistry teacher;
   Mr Dutch does not teach any course that is taught by Karl or Mr Painter.
   What is the full name of each teacher and which two subjects does each one teach?

2. How many statements from the list below are false?
   (a) Exactly one statement on this list is false.
   (b) Exactly two statements on this list are false.
   (c) Exactly three statements on this list are false.
   (d) Exactly four statements on this list are false.
   (e) Exactly five statements on this list are false.
   (f) Exactly six statements on this list are false.
   (g) Exactly seven statements on this list are false.
   (h) Exactly eight statements on this list are false.
   (i) Exactly nine statements on this list are false.
   (j) Exactly ten statements on this list are false.

3. A traveller is on his way to London. He reaches a fork in the road where he can either turn left or right. He knows that only one of the two roads leads to London, but he does not know which one. Fortunately, he sees two brothers standing at the fork, and he decides to ask them for directions. The traveller knows that one of the two brothers always tells the truth and the other one always lies. Unfortunately, he does not know which one always tells the truth and which one always lies. How can the traveller find out the way to London by asking just one question to only one of the two brothers?

4. At a family party, a grandfather, a grandmother, two fathers, two mothers, four children, three grandchildren, one brother, two sisters, two sons, two daughters, one father-in-law, one mother-in-law, and one daughter-in-law, sit at a table. At least how many people are sitting at the table?

Hint: Try and work out the relationship of each person by drawing a family tree.

5. You are a participant in a quiz. The quizmaster shows you three closed doors. He tells you that behind one of these doors, there is a prize, and behind the other two doors, there

is nothing. You select one of the doors, but before you open it, the quizmaster deliberately picks out a remaining empty door and shows that there is nothing behind it. The quizmaster offers you a chance to switch doors with the remaining closed door. Should you stick to your choice?

Hint: While this may seem like a simple yes or no question, analyse the logic behind your choice. Use simple maths to deduce your answer.

Exercise 2: Morse Code

Focus: Analytical Skills
Time: 10 minutes
Materials required: Paper and pen/pencil
Level: Expert

Morse Code was developed by Samuel Morse in the 1840s to send messages over the electric telegraph that he invented in 1836. The idea was that the electrical signals would punch marks on paper tapes in either dots or dashes. Today, Morse Code is used only for navigational radio beacons, amateur radio operators and land mobile transmitter identification. Here are the letters for Morse Code. Use them to decipher the sentences below.

A .-	J .- - -	S ...
B -...	K -.-	T -
C -.-.	L .-..	U ..-
D -..	M - -	V ...-
E .	N -.	W .- -
F ..-.	O - - -	X -..-
G - -.	P .- -.	Y -.- -
H	Q - -.-	Z - -..
I ..	R .-.	

1. The first message ever sent over the electric telegraph
    wire (four words):

    .- - .... .- -/.... .- - - ..../- -. - - - -../.- - .-. - - - ..- - -. ....
    -/

2. Popular nursery rhyme (four words):

    .-- ....-.. .../- - - -./- .... ./-... ..- .../

3. Secret message between two friends (four words):

    - - . . -/.- -/..-. - - - .. .-./.--. - -/

4. A mother has hidden the front door key for her daughter
    who is not home and doesn't have one. She has left her
    this message (four words):

    .-.. - - - - - - -./..- -. -.. . .-./- .... ./- - .- -/

5. A popular idiom when you're going through a tough
    time (six words):

    . ...- . .-. -.--/-.-. .-.. - - - .. -../.... .- .../.-/... .. .-.. ...- .
    .-./.-.. .. -. .. -. . - -./

Exercise 3: Hercules and Geryon's Cattle

Focus: Comprehension
Time: 15 minutes
Materials required: Paper and pen/pencil
Level: Expert

As mentioned in Week 2–Day 3, Hercules was given twelve tasks
by King Eurystheus to complete in twelve years so that he could
atone for the sin of murdering his wife and children. One of the
twelve tasks that Hercules was ordered to do was to capture the
cattle of the monster Geryon and bring it back to King Eurystheus.

Geryon was considered to be a monster and was rather odd
in that he had three heads and three sets of legs, all joined at
the waist. However, his oddity could be explained, given the fact
that his father Chrysaor had burst from the body of the Gorgon

Medusa after she was beheaded and his mother Callirrhoe was the daughter of two Titans, Oceanus and Tethys. Geryon lived on an island called Erythia, which was considered to be the end of the world but was actually near the boundary of Europe and Libya. Geryon's cattle was legendary and was guarded by a two-headed hound named Orthus and a herdsman named Eurytion.

Hercules set off on his long journey to the end of the world, undergoing and overcoming many trials along the way. When he finally reached the border, he built two massive mountains, one in Europe and one in Libya, to commemorate his long journey. These mountains became known as the Pillars of Hercules. The strait between these mountains is now called the Strait of Gibralter, between Spain and Morocco, the gateway from the Mediterranean Sea to the Atlantic Ocean.

When Hercules arrived at the island of Erythia, he was attacked by Orthus, whom he killed with his club. He dealt with Eurytion in the same way. When Hercules was trying to escape with the cattle, Geryon attacked him. A long fight ensued and Hercules shot and killed him with his arrows.

Hercules encountered many troubles on his way back to Greece with the cattle. Two sons of Posiedon, the god of the sea, tried to steal the cattle in Liguria and Hercules had to kill them. A bull escaped in Rhegium and jumped into the sea. It swam all the way to Sicily and journeyed through to the neighbouring country. The native word for bull was 'italus'; the country came to be called Italy. The bull was then captured and taken to King Eryx, another son of Poseidon, and put into his herd. When Hercules finally found the bull after a long search, Eryx refused to give it to him. On further persuasion, Eryx agreed to return the bull only if Hercules could beat him in a wrestling match. Hercules agreed and beat Eryx three times, killing the king in the end. He then returned the bull to the herd.

When Hercules was almost home, Hera once again stepped in to make life miserable for him. She sent a gadfly to bite the cattle, irritate them and attack the herd till they scattered far and wide. It took Hercules a very long time to find all the cows and regroup them, but he finally managed to do so and brought the cattle to Eurystheus, who then sacrificed the herd to Hera to appease her.

1. Describe Geryon.
2. Who were the monster, Geryon's parents and grandparents?
3. Who guarded Geryon's cattle?
4. What are the Pillars of Hercules and how were they formed? Where are they located?
5. What were the problems that Hercules encountered on his way back to Greece?
6. How did Italy get its name?
7. Write down in your own words, the sequence of events from the time Hercules reached Erythia till he returned to Greece.
8. After completing all twelve tasks, Apollo makes Hercules immortal, as promised. Do you think this is fair given that the tasks were meant as punishments for killing his family? Justify your answer.
9. In your opinion, what do you think is the moral of this story?

What are the meanings of the following words?

1. Titans
2. Gorgons
3. Italus
4. Gadfly

Exercise 4: Word Wheels

Focus: Language
Time: 10 minutes
Materials required: Paper and pen/pencil
Level: Expert

How many words of *four or more* letters can you make from the following word wheels?

Rules:

1. Every word must contain the central letter.
2. There must be at least one seven-letter word per word wheel.
3. You must find four or more words per word wheel.

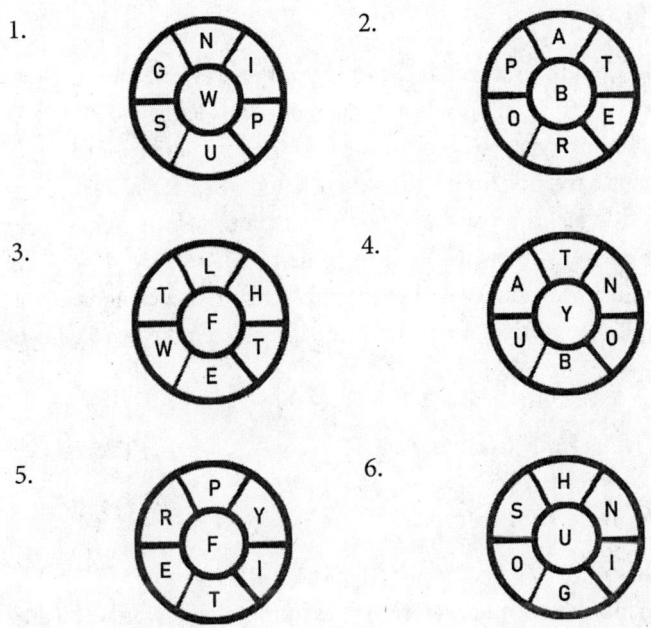

1.

2.

3.

4.

5.

6.

7.

8.

9.

10.

Scoring:

- Add up all the words individually for each word wheel. Give yourself 10 points for every correct seven-letter word and 5 points for every correct four-, five- and six-letter word.
- If you have not found the seven-letter word for a particular word wheel, or you have fewer than four words per wheel, the entire word wheel is disqualified.
- If you have not used the central letter or have made up a word, that particular word is disqualified from the word wheel.

Exercise 5: Kakuro

Focus: Numerical Reasoning
Time: 20 minutes
Material required: Pen/pencil
Level: Expert

Kakuro puzzles are often referred to as number crosswords and are more challenging than Sudoku puzzles. The aim of the game is to fill all the blank squares in the grid with only the numbers 1 to 9 so that the numbers you enter add up to the corresponding clues.

Kakuro puzzles contain many clue squares, which help you solve the puzzle. A clue square can have an 'across' clue or a 'down' clue, or both. The across clue is the number that is on the top-right corner and the down clue is the number on the bottom-left corner. The aim is to fill up the squares *adjacent* to the across clue with numbers that add up to the clue and to fill up the squares *below* the down clue so that the numbers add up to the clue.

For example, look at the sample puzzle below. As you can see, the number 9 is the 'down' clue, and therefore, all the numbers below the number 9 need to add up to 9. Number 4 is the 'across' clue, which means that all the numbers adjacent to the clue have to add up to the number 4. Numbers within a block must not repeat. For example, the numbers that add up to the number 9 cannot be 7 + 1 + 1.

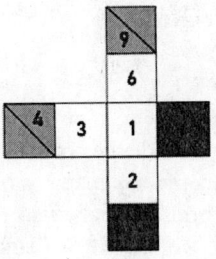

Try working out the following Kakuro puzzle in twenty minutes or less.

Hint: Start with a clue for which you know the answer to some certainty. For example, if the clue is the number 3, you know that the adjacent two squares can only have two options of 2 + 1 or 1 + 2.

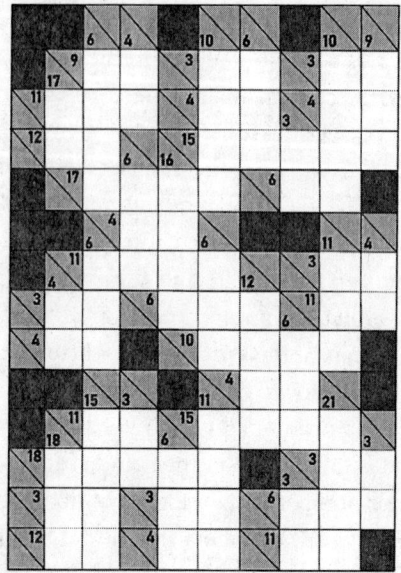

Exercise of the Day: The Artist Within

Time: 20 minutes

Many people give up drawing soon after leaving school since they have neither the confidence nor the time to develop their artistic abilities. However, no matter how good or bad you think you are, your brain will always benefit from anything that you try to draw, whether it is a simple doodle or a full picture.

Spend the next ten minutes drawing anything that you like. It can be geometric shapes, lines, doodles, spirals, people, letters, etc. Just let your mind wander with your pen or pencil and see what happens.

Now spend ten more minutes drawing with your 'other' hand. In other words, use your non-dominant hand to draw something.

Don't judge yourself or your drawing. Simply focus on the task at hand and enjoy it.

Chapter 16

Week 2—Day 7

Today, the focus is on active observation, lateral thinking, creativity, imagination and mindfulness.

Exercise 1: Active Deduction

Focus: Active Observation
Level: Expert

Sherlock Holmes's extraordinary talent for deduction is well documented by Sir Arthur Conan Doyle. Though they often seem nearly mystical in origin, Holmes's deductions were in fact the product of a keenly-trained mind. For example, the first time he meets Dr Watson, he says, 'You have been in Afghanistan, I presume'. He goes on to explain, 'Here is a gentleman of a medical type, but with the air of a military man. Clearly an army doctor, then. He has just come from the tropics, for his face is dark, and this is not the natural tint of his skin, for his wrists are fair. He has undergone hardship and sickness, as his haggard face says clearly. His left arm has been injured. He holds it in a stiff and unnatural manner. Where in the tropics could an English army doctor have seen much hardship and got his arm wounded? Clearly in Afghanistan.'

Today's active observation challenge might seem simple, but it requires all your powers of observation and deduction. As Sherlock Holmes himself says in *The Hound of the Baskervilles*, 'The world is full of obvious things which nobody by any chance ever observes'. Your task for today is to sit in a crowded place, maybe a coffee shop, your school field, your office, a bus stand or a metro station, and simply observe unknown people. Take any five random people, observe every detail about them and make deductions based on these observations (don't stalk them though!). Try and guess their profession, whether they are married, have pets, etc. Here are a few tips for you to follow:

1. Observe every little detail.
2. Pay attention to the basics.
3. Use all your senses.
4. Be 'actively passive' while talking to someone. This means paying attention to everything that the person is saying in addition to paying attention to every detail about the person's appearance, demeanour, etc. Paying attention to the person also means not fidgeting with your phone or any other gadget while having a conversation.
5. Based on what you observe, try and make deductions as accurately as you can.

Challenge: Try and continue this exercise throughout your life, observing every aspect of one person every day. Whether you're stuck at a traffic light or bored at a party, this would be a good way to entertain yourself while training your brain at the same time.

Exercise 2: Out-Of-The-Box Puzzles

Focus: Lateral Thinking
Time: 15 minutes
Material required: Pen/pencil
Level: Expert

The following puzzles and brain teasers may not have all the clues needed to solve them. Your task is to think outside the box, and come up with creative solutions.

1. The three houses below need to be supplied with three utility services namely, water, electricity and internet. Each house needs to be connected to all three utilities. This means that each house will have three lines and each utility will have three lines. The challenge is to connect them without crossing lines through houses or utilities. The houses cannot share lines either. Draw nine lines connecting the three houses to the three utilities.

Hint: Look at this puzzle as a three dimensional puzzle rather than a two-dimensional one.

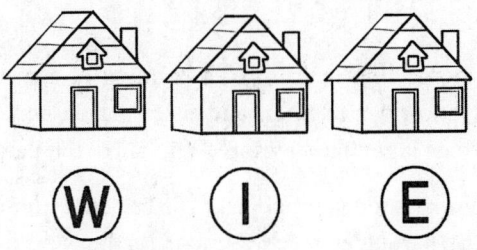

2. Nine dots are placed in three rows with three dots in each row as shown in the picture. These nine dots must be connected by four straight connected lines, without lifting up your pen.

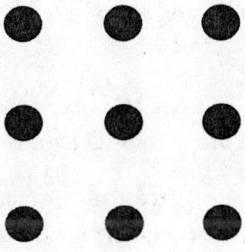

3. Fill up the following grid entirely with the remaining two letters of the alphabet such that each letter appears only once in the entire grid.

Note: There are 26 letters of the alphabet and 30 squares in this grid. Each square needs to be utilized.

B	D	I	C	H	K
J				O	P
X			A	G	Q
V	R		W	Y	U
S	E	N	M	F	L

4. A man is standing in front of a painting of a man and he says the following: 'Brothers and sisters have I none, but this man's father is my father's son'. Who is on the painting?

5. A man walks into a bar and asks the bartender for a glass of water. The bartender reaches under the bar and brings out a gun and aims it at the man. The man says thank you and leaves happily. What happened?

6. Anthony and Cleopatra are lying dead on the floor of a villa in Egypt. Nearby is a broken bowl. There is no mark on either of their bodies and they were not poisoned. How did they die?

7. A man pushed his car. He stopped when he reached a hotel at which point he knew he was bankrupt. Why?

8. Five pieces of coal, a carrot and a scarf are lying on the lawn. Nobody put them on the lawn but there is a perfectly logical reason why they should be there. What is it?

9. Based on a true story: Deep in a burnt forest was found the body of a man who was wearing only swimming trunks, snorkel and facemask. The nearest lake was 8 miles away and the sea was 100 miles away. How had he died?

10. A woman had two sons who were born on the same hour of the same day of the same year. But they were not twins. How could this be so?

Exercise 3: Sing-Song Chores

Focus: Creativity
Time: 10 minutes
Level: Expert

Make up a song to remember all the chores that you need to do today. You can either make up your own tune or use an existing tune. The song can be of any length. Your chores are:

1. Wash the dirty dishes in the sink
2. Buy groceries
3. Get the hole in your pants mended
4. Iron clothes
5. Organize and tidy up your cupboard
6. Cook something healthy
7. Read a homework assignment
8. Wash your vehicle
9. Clean the bathroom
10. Put things back in their places (clear up the living room)

Exercise 4: Mars Mysteries

Focus: Imagination
Time: 10 minutes
Materials required: Paper and pen/pencil

Level: Expert

You land on Mars and find a series of caves. While exploring them, you find skeletons which you assume are Martians but later find out are pre-historic humans from Earth. Write a story of any length (more than ten lines at least) describing your adventures on Mars.

Exercise 5: The Body Scan

Focus: Mindfulness
Time: 15 minutes
Level: Expert

Read all the instructions first before attempting this exercise.

1. Lie down flat on your back with your feet slightly separated and your palms facing up. If this is difficult for you or not possible where you currently are, sit on a chair with your feet firmly on the ground and your palms facing upwards on your thighs.

2. Lie very still or sit very still for the duration of the entire exercise. If you absolutely need to move, do so slowly and consciously.

3. Breathe normally. Breathe consciously, noticing the rhythm of your breath and the experience of breathing in and out. Do not change the rhythm of your breathing in any way; just be aware of the air being inhaled and exhaled from your nostrils, the rise and fall of your chest and abdomen and the quality of the air that you are breathing.

4. Now, move your attention to your body. How does the texture of your clothes feel on your skin, how does the texture of the mat that you are lying down on or the

chair that you are sitting on feel on your body, how is the temperature of your body and the environment around you and so on.

5. Pay attention to any part of your body that is tingling, sore, or feeling particularly heavy or light.

6. Start your body scan, beginning from your head and moving down to your toes. Be aware of each part of your body as you move downwards stopping at each part for about five seconds to ten seconds before moving on. If you like, you can clench that part of the body tightly for five seconds before letting go completely. This is the order that you can follow:

Face and head (forehead, eyebrows, eyes, nose, cheeks, mouth and jaws)
Neck
Shoulders
Chest
Arms (lower and upper parts, and elbows)
Hands (fingers, palms and wrist)
Abdomen
Pelvic region
Thighs
Knees
Lower legs
Feet
Toes

7. Once your body scan is complete and you are ready, slowly come back to the room and listen to the sounds around you. Open your eyes slowly and pay attention to the room that you are in.

Exercise of the Day: Journaling

Today's exercise of the day is not so much an exercise for today, but something that you can try and do throughout your life—keeping a journal. You can write anything that you want in your journal. Try and use a notebook and a pen rather than typing things out on your phone or on your computer. Take about 15 to 20 minutes every day to write about your day. You may think that this is counterproductive to developing a good memory but the reverse is true—writing things down actually activates the reticular activating system of your brain and enhances your learning capabilities. Start writing today. Make it a habit to write every day.

Congratulations on completing your first two weeks of brain training! The exercises of the last two weeks were just a start on your journey towards better brain health. Don't stop here! Make sure that you continue doing such exercises everyday so that you keep your brain healthy and active and stave off the effects of ageing and brain deterioration. Work out the puzzles every day in newspapers and download (and use!) brain training applications on your phone or on your computer. If you liked a certain type of puzzle in this book, Google it and try and find a website that has more of these puzzles. Of course, don't just stick to what you like; branch out into other puzzles as well with different levels of difficulty. The idea is to keep challenging your brain, not becoming comfortable even with brain training.

On the same lines, Part II of this book focuses on a set of exercises called Neurobics, which help you change up your routine on a daily basis while training your brain at the same time. Modify these exercises according to your own lifestyle, but make sure that you practise at least three of these exercises on a daily basis. Read on, to find out more about Neurobics.

PART II

Chapter 17

Neurobics

Neurobics is a new science of mental exercises that enhance the brain's performance. It was pioneered by Dr Lawrence C. Katz of Duke University, North Carolina. It is a unique science connected with brain training and is surprisingly simple and easy to put into action on a daily basis. It covers a broad spectrum of activities, drawing on some previously known ideas and then adding supplemental activities to the core ideas.

Earlier, it was believed that brain cells were fixed and that you had a given number when you were born. However, this new research in brain activity shows that the brain, like other parts of the body, produces new cells that adapt and become integrated in the brain's overall function. Neurobics is the first and only program to be scientifically based on the brain's ability to produce natural growth factors called neurotrophins that help fight off the effect of mental ageing. This research then branched out into producing specific activities that stimulate brain activity.

Your brain is naturally hardwired to seek out new and novel experiences that are stimulating and exciting. However, too much change and novelty can be quite unsettling, which is why you may settle into a routine that is dependable and comfortable. As mentioned in Chapter 1, routine is a double-edged sword and it can be good as well as bad for you. It can be good because it is comfortable, but could become bad for your brain since it encourages the repetition of the same thing over and over again. Therefore, it does not stimulate new neural connections.

This is where Neurobics comes in. Neurobic exercises use your five physical senses as well as your emotions in unexpected ways, and help you shake up your daily routines. These exercises basically enable you in continuing with your daily routine, with just a few minor adjustments or tweaks here and there. You do not need to take time out of your day just to do these exercises, rather, you can incorporate them into your daily routine. You can do them anywhere, anytime in offbeat, fun and easy ways while you're waking up, commuting, working, eating, shopping or relaxing. They are designed to help the brain manufacture its own nutrients that strengthen, preserve and grow brain cells.

Something as simple as applying your toothpaste and brushing your teeth with your non-dominant hand is a typical neurobic exercise. Even a small task like this would be considered as a brain exercise because it activates neural pathways that were previously unused or underused. This strengthens nerve connections and helps them stay young, strong and agile.

Different parts of your brain are activated by each of your senses—vision, hearing, smell, taste and touch. Most often, you may use your sense of sight and sound more than your other senses. This hones these senses but dulls or reduces the effectiveness of your remaining senses. Neurobics helps you utilize all your senses, giving importance to all five senses as well as your emotions, so that you activate different parts of your brain. This will help sharpen all your cognitive processes and help you think like a memory genius. (As mentioned in Chapter 1, the only difference between the brain of a memory genius and the brain of a 'normal' person is that a memory genius activates more parts of his brain while problem solving than a 'normal' person does.)

Dr Katz's research group found that relatively brief periods of brain exercise lasting less than an hour each day for only a week or two, can significantly increase the neural networks in the brain. In addition to mental exercises, it is essential to be physically fit and active and to keep your stress levels in check while taking care of your body's nutritional needs as well. Although this is a relatively new field, there is enough scientific evidence to prove the effectiveness of these techniques to help you keep your brain fit and active as you grow older.

Benefits of Neurobic Exercises

Your brain is one of the most vital organs of your body. Keeping it in shape is extremely important for people who hope to live long and healthy lives. The following are some of the known, scientifically proven benefits of neurobic exercises.

1. Neurobic exercises help increase the longevity of your brain, enabling it to function on a higher level, not just on a daily basis but as you grow older as well.

2. It increases the functionality of your brain so that you will be able to tackle more difficult tasks at a faster rate. It makes your brain more efficient while making it healthier.

3. Neurobic exercises provide a fun, innovative and easy way to help you improve your brain activity and better yourself in the long run. They do not require a specialized set of tools or intelligence, nor do they require you to take time out of your day in order to practise them. They can be easily incorporated into your schedule.

4. Research suggests that by practicing Neurobic exercises, you would be able to reduce the onset of brain degenerative diseases such as Alzheimer's disease and Parkinson's disease. You would also be able to slow

down the progress of these diseases if they have already developed.

5. Neurobic activities increase the overall health of your brain itself.

6. These exercises are designed to activate (mostly) the right hemisphere and the left hemisphere of your brain and sometimes both hemispheres together! Since more parts of your brain get stimulated and activated, more neural pathways are formed within your brain.

What Makes an Exercise Neurobic?

Neurobic exercises involve getting your brain out of its comfort zone by exposing it to new sensations or challenges that are out of the routine. You use all your senses to some extent right through the day. You also encounter new stimuli on a daily basis. However, dealing with these would not be considered to be neurobic exercises. For example, if you normally write with a black-ink pen and you decide to write with a blue-ink pen instead, it would not be considered as a neurobic exercise. Similarly, if you normally take the train but decide to take a taxi one day, it does not count as a neurobic exercise. What *would* be considered as a neurobic activity, however, is switching hands while writing (black-ink or blue-ink pens don't really matter) and writing with your non-dominant hand, or trying a new route to work that you haven't used before instead of taking the train. Both these activities will help you become more alert and observant, and you will become more aware of the processes involved in doing something different. Sure, writing with your non-dominant hand might be frustrating and difficult, and you may get lost on your way to work while trying out a new route, but either way, you would have activated a portion of your brain which you would not have previously used for these two activities and *that's* what is important.

Neurobic activities can be *physical*. This could involve changing some kind of action that you normally do or exposing yourself to new physical challenges or situations that involve not only your muscles working differently, but changing how your brain thinks of the body.

Neurobic activities can be *emotional and mental*, which involves changing the way you think or feel about something. Mental neurobics can involve counting, checking ones memory with little games, trying to think in a foreign language, etc. Here, the point is not to test your brain in something you are already good at, but rather to keep challenging your brain to do something that it has never done before in order to solve or tackle a new situation.

Neurobic exercises are *sensational*, which means that they make use of some or all of your five senses at the same time. This involves switching up the things you feel, taste, smell, hear, and see. By doing this, your brain will be able to deal with a wider variety of feelings, including stress and pain.

So, what are the conditions that make an exercise Neurobic? It *must* be one or more of the following:

1. Involve one or more of your senses in a novel way, perhaps including your emotions as well. By purposely not using the sense that you normally would use, you automatically force yourself to rely on other senses to do an ordinary task. For example, having a bath with your eyes closed and operating by your sense of touch alone. Here, you are purposely dimming your sense of sight but also honing your sense of touch in the same activity. You can also combine two or more senses in unexpected ways. For example, listen to music and eat

at the same time, but pay attention to both the music and your food. This combines your sense of taste as well as sound.

2. Get out of auto-pilot mode. When you follow a routine, you start doing things without thinking too much. However, when you change things, you wake your brain up and activate it enough to think about how to go about doing this new activity. The activity that you choose needs to be unusual, fun, surprising, able to engage your emotions, or must have some meaning for you. For example, taking a new route to work rather than taking the train. This activates your navigational skills (spatial memory), your processing speed, your semantic memory (information on various roads and one-ways, etc.) and your problem-solving skills—skills that you would not ordinarily use on a daily basis for this particular activity.

3. Break a routine activity in an unexpected, non-trivial way. Doing something new just for the sake of doing something new is not necessarily a neurobic activity. The activity itself needs to activate different senses, which in turn will trigger various cognitive functions of the brain. Rather than buying all your groceries from the supermarket, try buying them at a farmers' market or from individual stores. While this might seem like an unnecessary hassle and a roundabout way of buying groceries, you will exercise your brain in at least thinking of other possible locations where you would get fresh groceries and you would learn something new in the process.

While there is no 'best time' to practise neurobic exercises (any time is good), try to incorporate at least three to five neurobic activities into your daily schedule. You can incorporate the exercises into your morning routine, commute to work, mealtimes, leisure times, social activities, bedtime routines and, specifically, any time that you find yourself feeling bored. The main purpose is to switch routine things up a bit and make them more interesting and thought provoking.

SUMMARY

- Neurobics enhances the brain's performance by using five senses and your emotions in unexpected ways. This activates different parts of your brain and sharpens all your cognitive processes.
- Neurobics can be inculcated in your daily routine, whether you are waking up, eating, commuting, working, shopping, relaxing, etc. You do not need to take time out during the day just to do these exercises.
- Benefits of neurobic exercises include increasing the longevity of your brain while enabling it to function on a higher level, increasing the functionality of your brain to tackle difficult tasks, reducing the onset of brain degenerative diseases such as Alzheimer's disease and Parkinson's disease, increasing the overall health of the brain itself while activating both its right hemisphere as well as the left hemisphere.
- Conditions that make an exercise neurobic:
  - It must involve one or more of your senses in a novel way.
  - It must help you get out of auto-pilot mode and break from routine.
  - It must break from routine in an unexpected, non-trivial way.

Chapter 18

50 Neurobic Exercises

Before you start neurobic exercises, it is important to note that to incorporate these exercises into your daily life, you need to be able to make it a lifestyle change. Just as health experts advise against fad dieting on one side and binge eating on the other, neurobic exercises cannot be completely ignored, nor can you view them as a 'crash course' or a quick fix. You need to incorporate these exercises into your daily schedule. Fortunately, your normal, ordinary routines present hundreds of opportunities to activate your senses in extraordinary ways. Not all exercises may be appealing to you, but pick the ones that you like and practise them. Try and apply the same exercises in various situations and contexts so that you are constantly switching things up rather than making the neurobic exercises themselves routine. Just as you wouldn't binge on food, don't try to use neurobic exercises for every activity all day long. Pick two or three things on a daily basis and stick to the theme, or mix and match two neurobic activities. Once you get the hang of it, invent your own neurobic activities that you can use every day (inventing your own activities itself is neurobic).

The following are some neurobic exercises that you can try every day. Keep in mind that these are just suggestions. You are free to modify them in any way you please, as long as you fulfil one or more of the requirements that make an exercise neurobic—involving one or more of your senses in a novel way, getting out of auto-pilot mode and breaking your routine activity in an unexpected, non-trivial way.

1. Morning rituals. Most people have a fixed morning routine that enables them to wake up, get ready and leave for school or work in much the same way every single day. At some point in time, these routines are performed on auto-pilot, without much thought. Brain imaging studies show that novel tasks activate large areas of the cortex. However, when these tasks become routine, the activity in the cortex reduces. Here are a few ways that you can switch up your morning routine. Don't try everything at the same time. Pick and choose what you would like to do every day.

   a. Vary the order in which you do your normal routine. If you usually eat your breakfast first and then get dressed, try having a bath first, get dressed and then eat your breakfast. If you usually check your phone as soon as you wake up, try brushing your teeth first and getting your breakfast started before checking your phone.

   b. Eat something different for breakfast every day. Try eating your breakfast with your non-dominant hand.

   c. Take a new route while walking your dog.

   d. Change the order in which you read different sections of the morning newspaper. For example, if you are used to reading the news first and then doing the crossword, try switching it around.

   e. Brush your teeth with your non-dominant hand. This includes unscrewing the toothpaste's cap and squeezing the toothpaste onto the toothbrush as well. Try this with other activities as well, such as applying soap or shampoo while bathing, combing your hair, shaving (but be careful!), applying make-up, buttoning your clothes and putting on your accessories such as earrings, etc. This exercise requires you to use the opposite side of your brain instead of the side that you normally use.

Consequently, all those circuits, connections and brain areas involved in using your dominant hand are inactive, while their counterparts on the other side of your brain are suddenly required to direct a set of behaviours in which they don't usually participate. Research has shown that this type of exercise can result in a rapid and substantial expansion of circuits in the parts of the cortex that control and process tactile information from the hand.

f. Have a bath with your eyes closed. Locate the taps, bucket, mug, soap, shampoo, etc., just by touch. You will begin to notice various textures of common things around you, including your own body that you wouldn't usually notice when you are 'looking'. Although this might look like a relatively mild task, it is dynamic in waking your brain up.

g. Use only one hand to button your clothes, put your shoes on, or get dressed. As a challenge, try using only your non-dominant hand.

h. Is there anything in your morning routine that you can do with your feet instead of your hands?

i. Without looking into your wardrobe, try and pick out clothes based solely on touch. For example, only silk clothes today, or mix and match smooth and rough clothes. You don't need to use your fingers alone—you can also use your cheeks, lips or even your feet to feel the fabric, since all these areas are packed with sensory receptors. This exercise gives your brain practice in distinguishing between fine textures.

j. Wear noise cancellation earplugs or headphones in the morning (but not while you're riding or driving!) to block out all noise. Since this blocks out your sense of hearing, your other senses may be heightened and you will be more aware of things around you.

2. Commuting. Navigation is connected to spatial memory which is our awareness of where things are in space and time. Many scientists believe that spatial memory is one of the primitive memories that we inherited from our ancestors. Perhaps, early cavemen relied heavily on their spatial memory to detect and avoid predators and other threats in their environment. In today's world, we use spatial memory to avoid accidents since we can gauge the location of other vehicles on the road in relation to us. Honing this skill will help you be a better driver or rider, help you have fewer accidents (or none at all!), make your eye-hand coordination better and make your motor movements more fluid. As you have seen from the exercises in Part I of this book, spatial exercises involve a mental manipulation of objects, even if the objects are not physically present.

a. If you drive to work, enter and start your car with your eyes closed (but open your eyes to drive!). Everything from locating your car, to unlocking it, getting inside, putting on your seatbelt, putting your key in the ignition and starting your car can be done with your eyes closed. While you're at it, try and locate familiar controls such as the radio button, windscreen wiper knob, air conditioning switch, etc., just by touch alone. Before you open your eyes again, slowly bring your awareness back to the car and the task at hand of driving to work.

b. Drive with your windows down and the music off. This applies if you're taking a taxi, bus or train. In this exercise, walking is the best. Opening the windows lets in a plethora of aromas and noises. You may hear a school's siren in the distance, an ambulance siren just behind you, children playing in a field, etc. You may smell the aroma of freshly baked bread as you pass by a bakery or the odour of petrol as you pass a petrol bunk. All these are sounds and aromas/ odours that you would usually miss if you had your windows up and your music on full blast. All these activate and stimulate the visual, auditory and olfactory centres of your brain simultaneously.

c. As mentioned earlier, take a different route to school or work. Avoid lanes that you already know but explore new roads. This aids your spatial memory as well as your semantic memory and enhances your powers of concentration, problem solving and processing speed.

d. If possible, try and exchange vehicles with a friend for just a day or so just to get the feel and experience of a different vehicle.

e. If you are usually the driver, request someone else to drive and you can move to the passenger side or the back seat. It is possible that you are too busy driving and may overlook many things outside. Someone else driving gives you the opportunity to practise your active observation skills.

f. Place a cup full of coins of different denominations in your vehicle. If you're in a car, you can place this in your cup holder. If you're on a bike, simply put a handful of coins into your pockets. While at a traffic light, place your hand into the cup or into your pocket and by feel alone, try and determine the denomination of the coins. You can try this with other small objects such as earrings, cuff links, etc. Because we normally distinguish objects from each other by looking at them, this exercise helps make the same distinction through touch instead.

g. Car pool whenever you can. Have a lively conversation with your fellow car-poolers. This not only encourages social interaction but also stimulates your brain through meaningful conversations and discussions.

h. If you are travelling by train or bus, close your eyes (but don't fall asleep!) and try and figure out where you are every time the train or bus stops. You should know the name of the station or the bus stop. With your eyes closed, use other cues such as the speed of the vehicle, the number of turns in the road, the sound of people getting on or off, etc., to visualize where you are. Try and interact with the people around you (open your eyes for this one!).

3. Mealtimes. Food is directly linked to most social activities. When we think of weddings, we don't just think of the celebrations but of the food as well. We celebrate birthdays with cake and special occasions and festivals with rich food. Meal times, especially dinner times, are also good opportunities for families to catch up on day-to-day events and what's happening in each other's lives.

At meals, our visual, olfactory, taste, tactile, and even our emotional/pleasure systems are in high gear, activating different areas of the brain. However, we often tend to make meal times dull, predictable and repetitive. We may often watch TV and eat, without really paying attention to what we're eating or we may eat the same breakfast every day or have a fixed schedule for what we eat each day. However, mealtimes offer you a chance to use all your senses in a healthy way. This can be done by changing how you eat, rather than what you eat.

a. Make mealtimes social. Instead of reading the morning

newspaper while eating breakfast or watching TV while eating dinner, focus on the person that you are eating with. Have the whole family sit down together to eat. If you're at school or work, try and eat with a group of friends or colleagues. At school or at work, swap lunches with your classmate or colleague. Try and sit with someone new or invite someone new to come eat with you.

b. Eat a meal in silence. This includes sharing a meal with a family member or a friend in absolute silence. It also includes keeping away all gadgets, books, etc., and focusing only on your food. You'll be surprised at how the food you taste and the things you hear are greatly enhanced! In the absence of verbal communication, your other senses will be automatically be enhanced.

c. Sit in a different place for each meal. Often, families have specific places at the table where each family member sits. At school or work, you may sit in the same place and eat every day. Whether it is just switching chairs at the dining table or switching your location itself, you take yourself out of your usual comfort zone and learn to make new associations with new locations and food.

d. Close your nose when you eat. Most of what you call taste, actually depends on smell. This is why you can't taste food when you have a cold as your nose is blocked. By closing your nose when you eat, you move your attention to the texture and consistency of the food, using your mouth and tongue.

e. Have a potluck. On a holiday, have each family member (including the youngest) decide what to bring to the table. Put all the food together and eat it as one meal. This may bring about some strange combinations such as white rice and chocolate sauce, but it doesn't hurt to try something completely different once in a while.

f. A trip down the memory lane. Certain foods bring about strong memories of our childhood or special occasions. Look for foods that rekindle childhood memories. Try recreating a recipe that your mother used to make when you were younger. Try recreating the first date that you had with your significant other.

g. Do something new. Why not eat what you usually have for breakfast at dinner time? Or change the order in which you eat your food—try eating dessert first and then your main course and then a starter. Have an indoor picnic at home, maybe on your balcony! Eat with your non-dominant hand. All these activities are perfect in activating your brain since these are all new experiences.

h. Enrich your senses. Have a candlelight dinner. Use scented candles. Use the good China occasionally, even if it is not a special occasion or even if you're alone. Enriching the sensory, social and emotional environment surrounding meals feeds your brain, even though you may not be aware of it at the time.

i. Novel food. Every now and then, try a food that you have never tried before. Go to a restaurant and order something that you have never eaten before. Try and cook something new at home.

j. Try ethnic food. Try cooking food from other cultures such as Japanese, Mexican, French, etc. While eating, listen to music from the same country. Accompanying the meal with appropriate ethnic music adds an auditory dimension to taste sensations.

k. Cook something from scratch. Chopping ingredients activates your tactile senses. Pay attention to the texture and feel of every ingredient. As you cook, inhale the aroma of all the ingredients being mixed together in the pot. Keep tasting the food, adding and adjusting the spices according to taste. Cooking something is a great way to activate all your senses at the same time.

4. Your hobbies. Whether you've finished your homework for the day or just come home from a hard day at the office, or just finished a huge project, everybody needs time to relax and refresh their mind. However, not all forms of relaxation are good for the brain. For example, binge watching your favourite show on TV not only eats up many hours of your time but actually dulls your brain down! Studies show that your brain activity when you are watching TV is much lower than when you are sleeping!

   a. Existing hobbies. Many of your hobbies or leisure activities may already be neurobic in nature. Try and find new ways to switch things up a bit with your existing hobbies. For example, if you are a musician, try and play a different musical instrument.

   b. Attend a creative workshop. It can be anything like glass painting, sketching, embroidery, cooking, baking, etc. Try and learn as much as possible about a new hobby or skill and then come home and practise it.

   c. Ride or drive aimlessly. Take your bike or car out and randomly take any road. Don't have a destination in mind—just drive/ride. Stop and explore anything that tickles your fancy. If you see an interesting shop, stop and go inside. If you see an interesting tree by the side of the road, stop and try and climb it or take artistic photographs of it.

   d. Try a group art project. Call all your friends together and try mixed-media art. You may be interested in painting while your friend might be interested in sculptures. See how you can combine the two (or more) art forms. Have one gigantic paper and you and your friends can try and paint one picture on it without consulting each other on the outcome.

e. Start a new hobby. Take up gardening, learn a new language, paint, learn a musical instrument, try carpentry, try fixing everything that is broken at home yourself, photography, start birdwatching, etc.

5. Travel. Vacations are a good way to break routine and try different things. There's no point travelling outside your country and eating at a KFC or McDonald's like you do in your own city or town anyway. Use your vacations to travel to new places, explore everything about the place, try the local food, shop at the local markets (not at the usual department stores that are all over the world), etc. At every turn, travelling can involve something new for your senses. Spatial maps used for everyday navigation are suddenly unusable and new ones must be constructed. The stress you may feel taking in new sights, sounds, foods, and a foreign language is actually your brain moving into high gear!

a. Go camping. Camping involves not only all your senses but your cognitive and physical abilities as well. Finding the camp site makes use of your spatial memory assembling your tent and starting a camp fire makes use of your processing speed, episodic memory (if you've done it before) and procedural memory, and cooking on a fire instead of a stove activates different areas of your brain that are underused. Also, you will have to learn how to deal with and survive the climate conditions, etc.

b. When you travel, try and do something different from what you normally do. If you like going to beaches, don't just sit on the beach all day, rent a cycle and explore the town, talk to the locals, talk to your waiters and find out what's good to eat, etc. The challenge is not just to go somewhere different, but to also do something different there.

c. Local language. When you travel, try and speak the local language. Before you travel, learn a few important phrases that you can use and try and converse with the locals in their own language. Don't be afraid to make mistakes. People are always happy to correct you if you say something wrong.

6. Be social. Studies indicate that a lack of social interactions has a negative effect on the overall cognitive functions. Make a plan to meet friends over the weekend (and follow through!). Make it a point to call and speak to at least one friend every day for about ten minutes or more. Write a letter to a friend (on paper, not e-mail), whether he or she is in the same city or not, and post it. Meet at least one friend once a week for coffee or for dinner or any activity.

7. Local projects. Try and get involved in local projects. There may be a project to clean up your local park or make it more pet friendly, or clean up the lake or help distribute food to people who live in slums, etc.

8. Read aloud with your partner or friend. Take it in turns to be the reader or the listener. Read anything, whether it's a newspaper or a storybook. This might be a slow way of getting through an article but when you read aloud or listen to someone reading, you actually use different brain circuits

than when you read silently 'in your mind'. On the social side, this activity can help you spend some quality time with your partner and can also give you both something to talk about apart from normal, everyday things.

9. Have a game night. Organize a game night with your family or your friends. The more people the better! Play group games such as Pictionary, dumb charades, etc. Try and add a twist to any of these standard games. A list of possible games and the cognitive functions that they train are presented in the Appendix of this book.

10. Learn sign language. Signing requires your hands to do something completely new—be solely responsible for communication. This also enhances your eye-hand coordination, motor coordination and language and interpretation skills needed to understand various signs. Sign language is challenging, complex and rich and requires integrating new types of sensory information to take the place of the usual auditory associations. Try communicating with people non-verbally for an entire day.

11. Punning. Make a pun by associating the sound of a word with something else in a humorous, unexpected way. Get together with your friends and see who can come up with the most puns for various things. Make it a fun group activity. Some examples of word play or puns:

    a. Never interrupt someone working intently on a puzzle. Chances are, you'll hear some crosswords!

    b. I'm a big fan of whiteboards. I find them remarkable (re-markable).

    c. King Arthur's army was too tired to fight because it had too many sleepless knights!

d. I asked my French friend if she likes to play video games. She said, 'Wii!'

e. The machine at the coin factory suddenly stopped working with no explanation. It doesn't make any cents!

12. Name that sound. Open up your senses to the world around you. When you go for a walk, listen to all the sounds around you. When you get home, write down all the different sounds that you heard. Throughout the week, record strange sounds or uncommon sounds on your phone. At the end of the week, ask your family or friends to guess what sound it is. You can use sound effects as well.

13. Mix it up at the gym. Instead of running on the treadmill, why not run outside? Instead of using a stationary bike, why not ride a real bicycle outside? Try and use noise cancellation headphones or earplugs while you are exercising to bring your focus to the way your body feels while it is moving, the various muscles that you are exerting, etc.

14. Just sit. Sit on a bench in public, close your eyes, and take in what happens around you. Let your mind free, associate by using the sounds and smells that you experience.

15. Master a new gadget or software. Learn to use a computer with a different kind of operating system or download a new software program and try and learn it without the help of a user guide. Try learning a new musical instrument, or operating a video camera, etc.

16. Practise typing. If you type on the computer keyboard with just two fingers, looking for each letter, typing becomes a long and laborious process. Practise typing with all your fingers. Learn where each letter and number is on the keyboard,

then close your eyes and visualize where each key is. If you already know how to type, try typing without looking at the keyboard at all. Here, you will be relying on your spatial memory to get you through.

17. Build something. Build something with your hands. It can be paper animals using origami, or something much more complex like building a birdhouse with scraps of wood. If you are not using power tools, try closing one eye while building something. Since you lose depth perception, your brain has to rely on new cues. You will then rely on your sense of touch and spatial skills to piece things together.

18. Grow a garden. Even if it is just one potted plant at home or an entire garden, gardening is a rich neurobic experience, mostly because you use all your senses in the process. You need to feel the earth, smell the flowers, taste the fruits, etc. You need to use some of your cognitive processes of planning and creativity to figure out where the optimal location for your plants are, how much water to use while watering them or how often you need to water them. Try planting a few vegetables such as tomatoes and potatoes at home.

19. Experiment with gardening. Play a gardening chance game. Whenever you eat an apple, a watermelon or grapes, experiment by planting the seeds in various places in one big pot, and try and guess the plants that begin growing there. Imagine digging up this pot one day and finding a gigantic watermelon there!

20. Draw something without looking at it. Ask someone to put several small items in a box. Pick one item without looking at it. Use your fingers to get an idea about the shape, the texture, the contours, etc. Picture it clearly in your head and

then draw it without looking at it. As a challenge, use crayons or coloured pencils to imagine or predict the colours as well.

21. Smell your spices. Ask someone to blindfold you and arrange all the spices such as cardamom, cloves, cinnamon, black pepper, etc., in a row in front of you. Ask the person to put each spice near your nose, one at a time, so that you can smell it. Try not to touch it. Try and guess it as accurately as possible by smell alone.

22. Mute the TV. This can be a fun activity to do with a friend. While watching something new, mute the TV and try to ad-lib the scene that's playing, changing it up completely. Try putting in your own words for each actor and make the scene as funny as possible.

23. Guess the ingredients. While eating, especially if you're eating something new, try guessing the various ingredients that you are tasting. Inspect your food. Use visual cues as well as taste and smell to guess what your food could be made from. Is it baked, fried or sautéed? This stimulates neural connections because although people eat, they do not use their powers of perception while doing so.

24. Speak in song lyrics. This is another fun activity that you can do with your friends, especially if they listen to similar music. Try and speak only in song titles or song lyrics for one whole conversation. The lyrics need to make sense in the context of the conversation; it cannot be random lyrics thrown at each other.

25. Take the longer route. If you have time on your way back from school or work, try and take the longer way home. Play a game with yourself. See how many bakeries, petrol

bunks, restaurants, supermarkets, etc., are on this new route as opposed to the route that you usually take.

26. Different styles. Wear your hair in a different style. Perhaps, dyeing your hair a different colour, adding streaks to it or highlighting it. Try a different style of clothing. Mix and match random clothes in your cupboard and see if the outcome is interesting.

27. Move your furniture around at home. Most people have lived in their houses long enough to know the 'lay of the land' in terms of where the furniture is placed and the layout of the house in general. Once you arrange your furniture, you seldom move it. This in itself is a routine. When you navigate your home keeping the locations of the newly arranged furniture in mind, you are using your spatial memory and also activating your brain to move out of auto-pilot mode.

28. When you're typing something on the computer, use a font that you've never used before. Change the size of the font as well. Once you finish typing out the whole document, change the font and size to what is required. Experiment with different fonts, colours and sizes. This challenges your visual processing and makes typing out an assignment more enjoyable.

29. New music. Listen to a different genre of music than you usually do, then use the Internet to learn three new facts about this new genre of music. Look for new music from artists that you like as well as unfamiliar artists. Watch the music videos to songs that you have only heard so far. Now close your eyes and listen to the same song and try and picture the music video.

30. New reading material. Make it a point to read a book that is different from the genre that you are used to. If you read only fiction, try reading non-fiction. If you read only detective novels, try switching to fantasy novels.

31. Turn off the lights. When you enter your house in the evening, don't turn on the lights. Try to do what you usually do with all the lights off and/or with your eyes closed. For example, when you enter the house, you may hang up your keys on a key rack and then remove your shoes. You may then leave your handbag or briefcase on the sofa and then go to the kitchen to make a cup of coffee. Try doing all this (except making the coffee) without lights on or with your eyes closed. If you wake up in the night to drink water or go to the bathroom, don't put on any of the lights.

32. Listen to a particular piece of music while smelling something nice. The music will excite your sense of hearing while the aroma—be it a flower, scented candle or incense—will arouse your sense of smell. The combination of the two activates different areas of your brain and makes associations between different senses that much stronger.

33. Avoid social media. Don't check any of your social media accounts for one week. Disable all notifications from Facebook, Twitter, Instagram, etc., for a week. Be aware of how much more free time you have now and try to spend it wisely. Instead of chatting with someone online, call them on the phone or better, meet them and talk to them face to face.

34. Avoid TV. While you're avoiding social media, you might as well try and avoid watching TV as well. You can always catch up on your favourite shows later. Use this time to catch up

on some house work or any other work that you have been procrastinating.

35. Walk backwards. If the idea of walking backwards in public is too much for you, try it at home. When you enter the house, walk backwards, ensuring that you don't trip or bump into any furniture along the way. Your mind will have to work twice as hard as usual to comprehend this action.

36. Play chess. Chess is one of the only games that activate all your cognitive abilities of planning, spatial memory, processing speed, working memory, creativity and visual processing as well as motor movements. This game has the ability of improving your overall memory as well as activating and stimulating all parts of your brain simultaneously.

37. Playdough. Get a ball of playdough or children's modelling clay and mould it into any shape or pattern that you want. Be as creative and imaginative as you like. Close your eyes and feel the texture of the clay in your hands. Try to mould it into a particular shape (heart shape, circle or square) without looking.

38. Observe and draw. Select a new person, place or thing to observe in great detail every day. Study your chosen subject closely. Later in the day, recall the subject by drawing it with as many details as you can remember.

39. Goodbye lists! Try and do all your daily errands and shopping without any lists. Before you leave the house, have a clear mental picture of all the things that you need to buy and all the places where they are found. Follow your mental map.

40. Read and write. Read an article in a magazine or in a newspaper. Once you are done, try and recall a minimum

of five points and write them down.

41. Learn a new vocabulary word every day. Find ways to use the word in conversation during the day.

42. Select a random sentence in a magazine or newspaper. Try to make a new story using the words in the original sentence.

43. Create your own jigsaw puzzle. Take an old family picture and stick it on cardboard. Once it dries, cut it into tiny, strange shapes and see how long it takes you to assemble it. To make it even more difficult, try this exercise with an abstract picture and cut the picture into very tiny pieces. Time yourself. Try the same puzzle again after one week and see if you can beat your previous time.

44. Create mini-experiments that heighten your perceptual skills. For example, have a friend lay out several objects of different sizes, shapes and textures on the floor. Keeping your eyes shut, try to identify the objects by touch alone.

45. Dismantle and assemble. Just as you dismantled a ball-point pen and reassembled it as part of your procedural memory exercise in Week 1–Day 5, try the same exercise with different objects. If you get stuck and don't know how to reassemble something, ask someone to help you or learn by watching online tutorials.

46. Toy shopping. Be a kid again. Go to a toy shop and look at all the different gadgets and toys that are there. Buy yourself a new toy that meets the requirements of neurobics.

47. Before you go to bed, replay your day in your mind. See if you can remember the key events of your day in reverse order.

48. Sky watch. Watch the sunrise and the sunset (but don't look directly the sun!). Notice the various hues of colours in the sky. Watch them change as the sun rises or sets. Look at the clouds. Use your imagination to see what shapes you can see in the clouds. What phase is the moon in? Can you see any distinct characteristics of the moon that you may have missed before?

49. Play brain games every day. Use any of the parameters used in this book every day and hone and train these skills through the day. Try and complete the daily crossword or Sudoku and Kakuro in the newspapers every day. Enrol yourself in online brain training programs that keep challenging your problem solving abilities. Download applications from Google Play Store or the App Store that help train your brain on a daily basis.

50. Read a play aloud. Assemble your friends, assign parts to each person and read a play aloud. Try to enact at least one scene and do it like a professional actor would. Get into the character that you are playing. What do you think this person's mannerisms would be? What kind of accent would he use? What kind of hairstyle would he or she have? Alternately, take up a serious play but read it in comical voices and see how the meaning of the whole play might change.

Make brain training a lifestyle change that needs to be sustained right through your life. Make the games as enjoyable and as fun as possible. Try to incorporate neurobics into everything that you do (but don't overdo it!) so that you are more aware of things around you. Break from routine and there is never a dull moment in your life.

Chapter 19

Now That You Have It, Maintain It

Congratulations! Now that you have completed all the challenges and have started incorporating some of the neurobic exercises into your daily schedule, you should be feeling as mentally fit as ever! Everything that you have been doing over the last couple of weeks has been designed to exercise your brain, encourage it to build new connections and to work more efficiently for you. You should be finding it much easier to memorize whatever you wish to remember and be taking far more interest in everything going on around you. You should also be feeling more alert and energized, especially if you have completed all the exercises in Part I of this book and have started incorporating some of the neurobic exercises into your daily routines.

In order to maintain and build on your new found mental agility, you need to keep challenging and stimulating that amazing brain of yours. However, as much as regular brain exercises help in preserving, protecting, training and building your brain power, they cannot work in isolation to protect the overall health of your brain. For this, you need to make certain lifestyle changes.

Lifestyle Changes

Researchers have uncovered nine key lifestyle factors that promote brain exercise and reduce the risk of brain ageing. These lifestyle changes in addition to mental exercises will aid in the overall health of your brain. They are:

1. Regulate your numbers

High blood pressure, heart disease and strokes are risk factors for dementia. Work with your doctor to control body weight, blood pressure, cholesterol levels and blood sugar levels. Make sure that you take your prescribed tablets regularly.

2. Nutrition

Just as your body needs healthy food, your brain needs to be well nourished as well. Make sure that you eat healthy foods and avoid binging on unhealthy foods. Drink plenty of water. Your brain does not have the capacity to store water. When your brain is working on a full reserve of water, you will be able to think faster, be more focused and experience greater clarity and creativity.

3. Manage environmental toxins

Scientists have long suspected that environmental toxins play a role in brain degenerative disorders, such as Alzheimer's disease, Parkinson's disease and multiple sclerosis. Two known neurotoxins are mercury and aluminium. Some foods such as some types of fish contain mercury while aluminium can be found in unfiltered drinking water, food additives, antacids, diarrhoea medications, dandruff shampoos and underarm antiperspirants. Two simple solutions for minimizing exposure to aluminium toxins are to drink filtered water and to read the labels on foods and personal consumer products to screen out harmful products.

4. Stay physically active

Physical exercise increases blood flow to the brain which brings with it oxygen and nutrients that are essential to healthy brain functioning. Physical exercise also increases the circulation of endorphins, a hormone proven to boost both mood and memory.

Make sure that you get plenty of physical activity right through the day. Research indicates that people who walk briskly every day develop better attention and improve their decision making skills! This shows the direct impact of physical exercise on the functions of the brain. Try and workout for a minimum of half an hour every day, or at least a full workout three to four times a week.

5. Manage your stress

When you are feeling stressed or you are in a stressful situation, your brain secretes corticosterone, which is the stress hormone. Prolonged exposure to this stress hormone affects the brain adversely and reduces the brain's capacity to learn and take in new information, which then affects your memory. It is important to learn useful coping mechanisms to deal with stress.

6. Lead a life of purpose

Living with purpose is about being actively involved in meaningful work. Whether you volunteer or get paid for your work, if the work engages you and makes you feel productive, you would be living a life of purpose. Even if you are unclear on what you would like to specialize in when you are in college, or what kind of profession you would like, try volunteering in an NGO or try doing something that is environmentally friendly such as participating in a garbage clean-up at your local park, etc. during your free time.

7. Lead a life of passion

Don't just walk; dance! Look at how to make everything around you exciting. Try and make even the dullest of tasks fun and entertaining. Follow your passions. Write, paint, sketch, learn to kick-box, swim, attend cooking classes, do whatever tickles your fancy. Keep trying new things, enjoy and have fun in everything that you do.

8. Connect with people

Stay socially connected to your friends and family. Nobody can live in isolation. Isolation is a huge risk factor for poor physical and mental health, depression and suicide. Studies have shown that social interactions create positive hormones in your body, which are good for brain health. Plan outings with your friends, try conversing with strangers while commuting, repair broken friendships, connect with your family, travel, join fitness groups or book clubs…connect!

9. Never stop learning

Learning new things continuously trains your brain while routines have the capacity to drain your brain. Regardless of your education, your educational level, or your age, it is never too late to break out of the routine and create new learning opportunities. Learning does not stop with school or college but is a lifelong pursuit. Make it a point to learn something new every day, whether it is a new word, or trivia or a new skill. Try and apply your new learning in different situations. Look for opportunities to learn new things. Attend workshops and conferences, talk to different people from different cultures and different professions, try and learn a new language, watch foreign language movies with the subtitles on, listen to new genres of music…the list can go on. Make it a point to continue learning all through your life.

Daily Plan

These are a few ways by which you can stimulate your brain on a daily basis:

1. Play games with your mind as you go about your daily

life, to keep it stimulated. You can turn any activity into a game by applying any neurobic exercise to it.

2. Play board games, card games or strategy games at least once a day, either on a gadget or with your friends or family.

3. Try to do at least one thing differently every day. This will reduce your brain's tendency to finish tasks on auto-pilot.

4. Get some fresh air and sunlight every day, and spend a few minutes' deep breathing or doing mindfulness exercises. This will keep you calm, relaxed, focused and refreshed.

5. Make sure to use some of the memory techniques described in Chapter 2 at least once every day. These are your core brain tools and they will help your mind perform at its best for you.

6. Solve the crossword puzzle and any other puzzles in your newspaper every day. Set aside time to do this activity. Once you master the basic crossword, try the cryptic version.

Weekly Plan

1. Once or twice a week, take at least five of the parameters that you have trained with (short-term memory, working memory, long-term memory, episodic memory, semantic memory, procedural memory, spatial memory, processing speed, logic and analytical skills, comprehension, language, numerical reasoning, active observation, lateral thinking, creativity and imagination) and work out problems associated with each of those parameters.

2. Once you finish them, try and make up your own problems and exercises related to each of the parameters. This will take your brain one step further—in addition to solving an exercise, you would actually be creating an exercise. You can

make this activity a social activity as well by inviting your friends to solve some of the exercises that you have created.

3. Make it a point to learn something new every week. Make it something big. For example, if you are interested in a particular topic, try and watch a documentary related to that topic or read up about it or discuss it with your friends. Pick a new topic every week.

4. Exercise for at least half an hour to an hour three times a week. Make physical exercise a top priority. Mix it up. Go to the gym on some days and walk or jog outside on others. Learn a new exercise every week and try and incorporate it into your exercise routine.

5. Set aside about fifteen to thirty minutes at least once a week to practise relaxation and mindfulness exercises. This will help calm you down after a long week and will also help you sleep better.

Annual plan

1. Once a year, take up a brand new interest or hobby and stick with it and practise it proactively for at least three months.

2. Revisit all the seventeen parameters in this book and train your brain in the parameters that you may have neglected over the last year. Work out similar exercises and see if you are able to do them faster than before.

Stick to the above maintenance plan of making changes in your lifestyle and having a daily, weekly and annual plan, and you should be able to age-proof your brain indefinitely. Even better, you should be able to develop and maintain your energy and vigour for life, even in your old age. With the kind of sharp brain and cognitive skills that you develop through life, you will well and truly be a force to reckon with in all aspects of your life.

SUMMARY

- Make training your brain a lifestyle change by keeping your blood pressure, cholesterol levels, etc., under control, following a good diet, managing environmental toxins, staying physically active, managing your stress, leading a life of purpose and passion, connecting with people and continuing to learn all through your life.
- Have a daily plan, a weekly plan and an annual plan to train your brain and keep your brain agile and fit.

Answers

Exercise 3: Baby Animals Crossword

M	O	L	E							
A			C		P	U	P	P	Y	
G			R		I		U			H
G	O	S	L	I	N	G		R		H
O		Q		A	L	A	R	V	A	
T		U			E					T
	C	A	L	F	T					C
H	A	B		A		F	I	S		H
	L		O	W	L		I			L
	V		N		I	N	K			I
H	E	N								N
	S		D	U	C	K	L	I	N	G

Exercise 5: General Knowledge Quiz

1. b
2. a
3. b
4. b
5. c

6. c
7. b
8. a
9. a
10. c

WEEK 1—DAY 2

Exercise 2: Spatial Puzzles

1. b
2. c
3. b
4. Both lines are the same length.
5. The water level falls. When the metal is taken out of the bowl, the bowl displaces less water. Therefore the water level falls by an amount corresponding to the volume of water equal to the weight of the metal. When the metal is dropped in the water, it displaces its own volume of water and the water level rises. The amount by which it rises corresponds to the volume of the metal, less than the volume of an equal weight of water. Therefore, the water level falls.

Exercise 4: Just Deduce It!

1. If Mary is the oldest and Sarah is not the youngest, then Elizabeth is the youngest.
2. True. If some Hocus Pocus are Alakazams and all Alakazams are Open Sesame, then some Hocus Pocus are Open Sesame.
3. c) Smriti
4. They're both standing back to back.
5. Ann was born in the year 2008 B.C.

Exercise 5: Riddle Me This

1. Why would the stranger knock if it was his room? He would have had a key! Knocking on doors is typical behaviour of criminals who break into hotel rooms to steal things. If nobody answers, they know that the room is empty and can break in unhindered.

2. A man who has just jumped out of a window can't stop to close it after him!

3. The internet did not exist in the 1960s, so he could not have watched a video online.

4. If the man checked between pages 5 and 6 and pages 1 and 2, it means that the book was numbered such that odd numbered pages were on the left while even numbered pages were on the right hand side. Pages 4 and 5 therefore would have been two sides of the same page. Therefore, the plumber was the thief.

5. When a window is broken from the outside by a thief, most of the glass will be found on the inside of the house, not on the lawn outside the house.

WEEK 1—DAY 3

Exercise 2: Word Circles

1. Zigzag
2. Quirky
3. Pyjama
4. Joking
5. Zombie
6. Puzzle
7. Jackal
8. Jumped
9. Jumble
10. Breezy

Exercise 3: Figure It Out!

1. a) $5 \times 30 - 23 - 9 = 118$
   b) $11 \times 11 + 11 = 132$
   c) $100 - 5 + 20 + 2 = 117$

2. a) The answer is 1. The sequence is subtract 4, divide by 2, subtract 4, divide by two... ($68-4=64$, $64÷2=32$, ...)
   b) 17. They are all prime numbers.
   c) 6. The third number in each sequence is the product of the first two numbers.

3. 30 squares. 16 squares (1 × 1) + 9 squares (2 × 2) + 4 squares (3 × 3) + 1 large square (4 × 4) = 30 squares altogether.

4.

The equation is:

b – c = a

b + c = d

(d+c) – (a+b) = e

5. 30 tickets

Exercise 4: Odd Four

The football, band aid, beehive and baseball bat do not have doubles.

Exercise 5: Out-Of-The-Box Riddles

1. Vinay is a dwarf. The first time that they go up, Akshay presses the button on the elevator for the eleventh floor. On the way down, Vinay is able to reach the ground floor button but on his way up again, he can only reach the eighth floor button and has to walk the rest of the way.

2. When Inspector Narayan searches their things, he finds their tickets in their travel itinerary. While the husband had booked two onward tickets, he had booked only one return ticket for himself but not for his wife. He had known that she would not be returning with him. Therefore, he was suspected of killing her.

3. The donkey is tied to a post and walks in circles around it, which is why his outer legs travel more than his inner legs.
4. My uncle is my father's identical twin brother.
5. Just put a stroke over the number one in the centre, making it a T like so: l0 T0 l0

WEEK 1—DAY 5

Exercise 4: Spatial Puzzles

1.

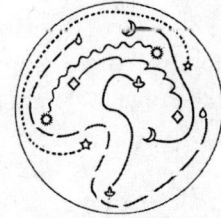

2. The coin puzzle can be solved in four moves as follows. Coins are numbered from left to right as shown below.
    a) Move 3, 4 to the right of 5 but separated from 5 by a gap equal to the width of two coins.
    b) Move 1, 2 to the right of 3, 4, with coins 4 and 1 touching.
    c) Move 4, 1 to the gap between 5 and 3.
    d) Move 5, 4 to the gap between 3 and 2.

If you would like to solve the puzzle without leaving gaps, it can be done in five moves as follows:
    a) Move 1, 2 to the right of 5.
    b) Move 3, 4 to the right of 2. (The coins will now be ordered as 5,1,2,3,4)
    c) Move 1, 2 again, to the right of 4 with 4 and 1 touching. (Order: 5 gap 3,4,1,2)
    d) Move 4, 1 back to the left to the gap between 5 and 3. (Order: 5,4,1,3 gap 2)

e) Move 5 and 4 to fill up the gap between 3 and 2.

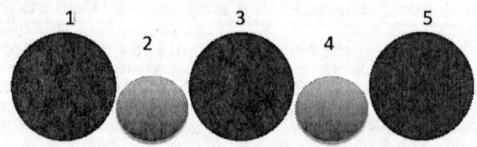

3. 1. No – This is easily seen to be a simple loop if you imagine
        the right hand loop moved to the left.
    2. Yes – This is the simplest knot possible.
    3. Yes
    4. No – The large loop at the bottom will slip through the
        hole in the middle, and this will become a straight piece
        of rope.
    5. Yes
    6. No
    7. No
    8. Yes
    9. No

WEEK 1—DAY 6

Exercise 1: Seating Arrangements

1. Praveen was sitting to the right of Aysha so Nikhil must
    have been sitting to her left. Since Mansi is Nikhil's wife,
    she would not be sitting next to him but either Kavery or
    Diya would be. Let's consider both cases.
    a) If Kavery was sitting to the left of Nikhil, then Sameer
        must have been sitting to her left (we already know
        where Praveen and Nikhil are sitting and Hari is Kavery's
        husband). We know that Diya was also sitting next to
        Sameer so she must have taken the seat to his left. The
        remaining two seats were occupied by Hari and Mansi

which means that Hari was sitting to the right of Mansi.

b) If Diya was sitting to the left of Nikhil, then Sameer sat to her left. The next three seats would have been occupied by Mansi, Kavery and Hari. Hari would have been between Mansi and Kavery (otherwise the two ladies would have been sitting next to each other). In that case however, Kavery would have been sitting next to her husband Hari. Since this scenario is then rejected, we go with answer a—Hari was sitting to the right of Mansi.

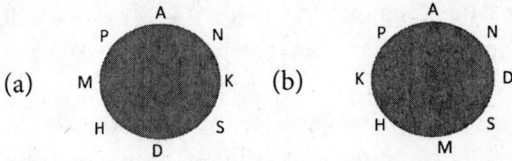

2. Ravi is sitting to Nisha's left in the front row.
Prakash is sitting behind Ravi in the second row.
We are already told that Rohan is sitting alone in the third row.
Vipin and Swathi are sitting in the fourth row in line with Ravi and Nisha.

3. We are told that two girls sat next to each other but Cauvery did not sit beside Diksha or Preethi. Therefore Diksha and Preethi were the two girls who were sitting next to each other. We are also told that Aakash was opposite Benny. Vinay sat to Cauvery's left and opposite Preethi. Therefore, their arrangement is as follows:

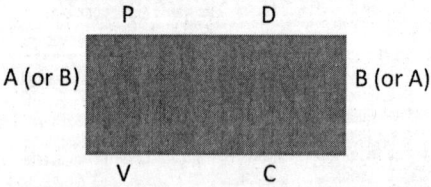

Exercise 2: Whodunnit?

1. The note said '? Anderson. He threw the snowball'. When you read the ? symbol out loud, you say 'Question Mark Anderson. He threw the snowball'. Mark Anderson was therefore the culprit who threw the snowball.

2. The seaman did it. The Japanese flag has a white background with a red circle in the centre. It looks the same, whether it is upside down or right-side up.

3. The elements written on the paper were Nickel, Carbon, Oxygen, Lanthanum and Sulfur. The abbreviations of these elements are Ni,C,O,La,S. Therefore, Nicolas was the murderer.

4. The police arrested the cook and John's wife. Why would he be making breakfast in the afternoon and why would she be waiting for her breakfast when it must have been lunch time?

5. The numbers 7, 10, 11, 8 and 9 that were circled on the calendar correspond to the months of the year July, October, November, August and September. When you take the first letter of each month, they spell JONAS. Therefore, Jonas was the murderer.

Exercise 4: Idioms

1. All brawn, no brain.
2. I'm over the moon.
3. Drop of a hat.

4. Just in time.
5. Beating around the bush.
6. Don't count your chickens before they hatch.
7. Heard it through the grapevine.
8. Bags under my eyes.
9. Let sleeping dogs lie.
10. On the ball.
11. Stealing one's thunder.
12. Head in the clouds.
13. Reading between the lines.
14. Storm in a teacup.
15. One tough cookie.

Exercise 5: Figure It Out!

1.

668	1	1332
1331	667	3
2	1333	666

2. a) Singapore – Tuesday 11:10 a.m.
      Mexico City – Monday 10:10 p.m.
   b) 10:30 p.m.
   c) 4:13 p.m.
3. A $(9 + 10 + 11) - (5 + 6 + 7) = 12$
   B $(8 + 9 + 10) - (1 + 2 + 3) = 21$
   C $(15 + 16 + 17) - (3 + 4 + 5) = 36$

WEEK 1—DAY 7

Exercise 1: Odd Three

The duck, clothes hanger and donut do not have pairs.

Exercise 2: Out-Of-The-Box Riddles

1. It was winter, and the river was frozen. The dog merely ran across the river.
2. The two men were not playing against each other.
3. She was in the Southern Hemisphere where the seasons are reversed.
4. Add a diagonal line on the top left of the first plus sign to convert + into a 4.
5. The other end of the rope was not tied to anything.
6. Put seven oranges in each of the first three bags and then put these three bags inside the fourth bag.
7. The poison was in the ice cubes inside the iced tea. Because the thirsty woman had drunk her iced tea very quickly, the ice did not have time to melt whereas the other woman nursed her drink and so the ice melted and released the poison into the drink.
8. The man is bald.
9. Only once. After the first time, the number does not stay 20 but decreases to 15 and then 10 and then 5...
10. 4 kids get an apple (one apple for each one of them) and the fifth kid gets an apple with the basket still containing the apple.
11. The man takes the sheep first (the fox will not eat cabbage). The man then returns and takes the fox to other side but takes the sheep back to the original side. He leaves the sheep and takes the cabbage to the other side. Then returns to the original side to take the sheep again to the other side.
12. He wants to pile up the dirt from his tunnelling and climb it so that he would be able to reach the unbarred window and climb through it to freedom.
13. Only I was going to St. Ives. I met all the others coming *from* the direction of St. Ives.

14. While the jury was looking at the door, the accused woman was looking at the jury and not the door. She knew that her husband would not be walking through because she had murdered him.

15. The poison was in the water, not the pills.

Exercise 5: Word Search

M	S	I	P	P	I	I	S	S	M	I	P	P
I	I	S	M	S	M	M	I	S	S	P	S	S
S	M	S	I	S	I	I	P	M	S	**I**	P	M
S	M	I	M	I	S	P	S	I	M	P	S	S
I	I	S	S	P	S	P	I	S	S	I	P	P
P	I	S	S	P	I	I	S	M	I	S	S	I
S	S	I	I	I	P	S	S	S	S	P	I	S
I	S	P	S	P	P	P	I	S	S	S	P	P
P	**I**	**P**	**P**	**I**	**S**	**S**	**I**	**S**	**S**	**I**	**M**	I
P	I	P	I	P	S	P	P	M	I	S	S	P
I	P	I	P	S	S	M	P	P	I	S	I	S
5	P	S	P	I	I	S	S	I	P	P	I	M
S	I	S	I	S	P	S	M	P	S	M	I	S

WEEK 2—DAY 1

Exercise 5: Your World

1. Six months
2. Dinosaur
3. Deciduous
4. United Kingdom and Zanzibar in 1896.
5. Abraham Lincoln

6. Dictionary
7. Louis Pasteur
8. Greenland
9. Czech Republic
10. The Hanging Gardens of Babylon
11. Switzerland
12. A Bishop
13. The Mona Lisa
14. Merchant of Venice
15. Edible seaweed
16. Barley
17. Bertie Wooster
18. Tennessee Williams
19. Franklin Roosevelt
20. Manchester
21. Country
22. By being out on the first ball
23. Ho Chi Minh City
24. What you see is what you get
25. Penicillin

WEEK 2—DAY 2

Exercise 2: Spatial Puzzles

1. 86
2. A movement of 42 teeth will see the T revolving completely 7 times and the R revolving completely six times, with the O remaining unaffected. The Y will turn $4^2/_3$ time around, and as the Y reads correctly every third of a turn, it will still read as a Y.
3. B is the correct answer. At each stage, the grey and black circles in the eclipse change places. The larger black circle

moves one place to the right at each stage so it ends up to the right of the eclipse.

Exercise 3: Odd Unscramble

1. Subjects in high school.
   a) Maths
   b) English
   c) Houses
   d) Science
   e) History

2. Types of trees
   a) Birch
   b) Bottle
   c) Banyan
   d) Pine
   e) Elm

3. Types of furniture
   a) Chair
   b) Cupboard
   c) Desk
   d) Textbook
   e) Dresser

4. Breed of dogs
   a) Poodle
   b) Siamese
   c) Boxer
   d) Dachshund
   e) Labrador

5. Continents
   a) Australia
   b) Antarctica
   c) Algeria

d) Europe

e) Africa

6. Different gases

   a) General

   b) Oxygen

   c) Helium

   d) Nitrogen

   e) Hydrogen

7. Types of flowers

   a) Daffodils

   b) Carnation

   c) Sunshine

   d) Violets

   e) Iris

8. Names of languages

   a) Greek

   b) Engine

   c) Spanish

   d) German

   e) Hebrew

9. Types of water bodies

   a) Rivers

   b) Lakes

   c) Seas

   d) Streams

   e) Clouds

10. House pets

    a) Rabbit

    b) Hamster

    c) Cheetah

    d) Goldfish

    e) Lovebird

Exercise 4: Out-Of-The-Box Riddles

1. They will name their baby Tiana. The pattern in the children's names are 'do, re, mi, fa, so, la, ti'(a system to learn musical scales) for **Do**nald, **Re**becka, **Mi**a, **Fa**ith, **So**nali, **La**yla and **Ti**ana.

2. a) You check the 16 year-old to see what he is drinking and you check the beer drinker to see how old he is.

   b) Most people answer that you need to turn over the card with a square on it and the blue card. In fact, the answer is to turn over the red card and the square. This is because the rule can be shown to be broken only if a card is found with a square on one side and red on the other (get some cards and try it for yourself).

3. We know that Martin tells the truth on only a single day of the week. If the statement on day 1 is untrue, this means that he tells the truth on Monday or Tuesday. If the statement on day 3 is untrue, this means that he tells the truth on Wednesday or Friday. Since Richard tells the truth on only one day, these statements cannot both be untrue. Therefore, exactly one of these statements must be true, and the statement on day 2 must be untrue.

   Assume that the statement on day 1 is true. Then the statement on day 3 must be untrue, from which follows that Richard tells the truth on Wednesday or Friday. Consequently, day 1 is a Wednesday or a Friday. Therefore, day 2 is a Thursday or a Saturday. However, this would imply that the statement on day 2 is true, which is impossible. From this, we can conclude that the statement on day 1 must be untrue.

   This means that Richard told the truth on day 3 and that this day is a Monday or a Tuesday. Therefore, day 2 is a Sunday or a Monday. Because the statement on day 2 must be untrue, we can conclude that day 2 is a Monday.

Consequently, day 3 is a Tuesday. Therefore, the day on which Richard tells the truth is Tuesday.

Exercise 5: Whodunnit?

1. There are five statements in which nothing is said about the possible offender: A1, A2, A3, B3, and C1.

The statements A1 and C1 seem to be contradictory, but that is not the case! Although at most one of these statements can be true, they can also be *both false*! For example, suspects A and C might only know each other from primary school.

About the statements A2 and B3, not much can be said (although it seems unlikely that statement A2 would be false and at the same time statement B3 would be true).

In addition, it follows from the introduction that statement A3 is true.

On the basis of an assumption about which suspect is the offender, we can count how many of the remaining statements are true:

Statement	A is the thief	B is the thief	C is the thief	D is the thief	None of them is the thief
B1	False	False	True	False	False
B2	False	True	True	True	True
C2	True	False	True	True	True
C3	False	False	False	True	False
D1	True	True	False	True	True
D2	True	True	True	False	True
D3	True	False	False	False	False
Total:	4 true, 3 false	3 true, 4 false	4 true, 3 false	4 true, 3 false	4 true. 3 false

Combined with the fact that Statement A 3 is true, this gives:

	A is the thief	B is the thief	C is the thief	D is the thief	None of them is the thief
Total	5 true, 3 false	4 true, 4 false	5 true, 3 false	5 true, 3 false	5 true, 3 false

Because the inspector knew that four statements were true, the statements A1, A2, B3 and C1 must be false and suspect B is the thief. Therefore suspect B was arrested.

WEEK 2—DAY 3

Exercise 2: Word Ladders

1. MOM
   MUM
   MUD
   MAD
   DAD

2. FALL
   TALL
   TOLL
   TOLD
   COLD

3. PIG
   BIG
   BAG
   BAY
   SAY
   STY

4. DRY
   DAY
   BAY
   BAT
   BET
   WET

5. WHEAT
   CHEAT
   CLEAT
   BLEAT
   BLEAK
   BREAK
   BREAD

6. COMB
   COME
   CAME
   LAME
   LAIE
   LAIR
   HAIR

7. PINK
   PINS
   PIUS
   PLUS
   FLUS
   FLUE
   BLUE

8. WHITE
   WHINE
   CHINE
   CHINK
   CLINK
   BLINK
   BLANK
   BLACK

9. COLD
   CORD
   CARD
   WARD
   WARM

10. HATE
    LATE
    LARE
    LORE
    LOVE

Exercise 3: Figure It Out!

1.

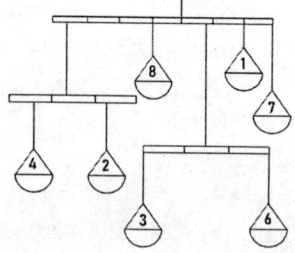

2. There are 880 solutions to this problem, if you leave out all rotations and mirror solutions. Here is one possible solution:

8	1	10	15
13	12	3	6
11	14	5	4
2	7	16	9

3. Just move the 6 up a bit like so: $2^6 - 63 = 1$
   Therefore, $2 \times 2 \times 2 \times 2 \times 2 \times 2 = 64$ and $64 - 63 = 1$

4. In 3 1/2 hours the alarm clock has become 14 minutes slow. At noon the alarm clock will fall behind approximately an additional minute. Its hands will show noon in 15 minutes.

5. The next number is a 2. This single sequence consists of two sequences: The first one is numbers 2-3-4-5 and the second is 9-18-36-72. To make the puzzle harder, all digits have been placed alternately.

Exercise 5: Riddles

1. A pair of shoes
2. Inkstand. 'Kst' is in the middle, 'in' is at the beginning and 'and' is at the end.

3. His father was 'in front of him' when he was born, therefore he was born 'before' him. His mother died while giving birth to him. Finally, he grew up to be a minister and married his sister at her wedding ceremony.

4. Ice.

5. The second hand on a clock or watch.

6. A dice.

   '1 to 6' are the numbers on all the faces of the dice,

   '15 to 20' is the sum of the exposed faces when the dice comes to rest after being thrown,

   'always 5' is the number of exposed faces when the dice is at rest,

   'never 21' is the sum of the exposed faces. It is never 21 when the dice is at rest.

   'unless it's flying' is the sum of all exposed faces when the dice is being thrown: 21 (1 + 2 + 3 + 4 + 5 + 6).

7. Your thumb.

8. A snowflake.

9. Words.

10. They were already facing each other to begin with.

WEEK 2—DAY 5

Exercise 4: Spatial Puzzles

1. The first sheet is folded as follows. Hold it face down so that when you look down on it, the numbered squares are in this position:

2	3	6	5
1	8	7	4

Fold the right half on the left so that the number 5 goes over the number 2, 6 on 3, 4 on 1 and 7 on 8. Fold the bottom half up so that 4 goes on 5 and 7 goes on 6. Now tuck 4 and 5 between 6 and 3, and fold 1 and 2 under the packet.

The second sheet is first folded in half, the long way, the numbers outside, and held so that 4536 is uppermost. Fold 4 on 5. The right end of the strip (squares 6 and 7) is pushed between 1 and 4, the bent along the folded edge of 4 so that 6 and 7 go between 8 and 5, and 3 and 2 go between 1 and 4.

2. Answer:

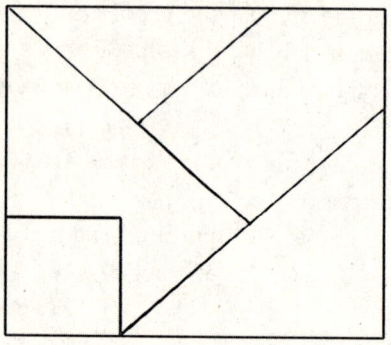

Exercise 5: A+ Word Search

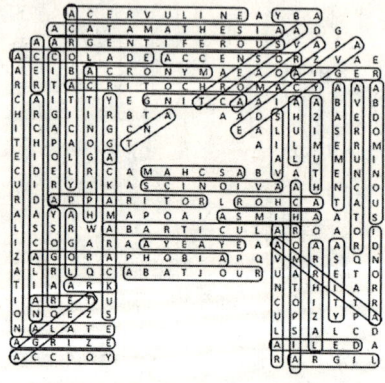

WEEK 2—DAY 6

Exercise 1: Just Deduce It!

1. Since Peter is the only one who does not teach the Dutch language, and Mr. Dutch does not teach any course that is taught by Karl or Mr. Painter, it follows that Peter and Mr. Dutch are the same person and that he is at least the maths teacher. Simon and Mr. English both teach history, and are among the three Dutch teachers. Peter Dutch therefore has to teach chemistry and maths. Because Steven is also the chemistry teacher, he cannot be Mr. English or Mr. Painter, so he must be Mr Writer. Since Karl and Mr Painter are two different persons, just like Simon and Mr. English, the names of the other two teachers are Karl English and Simon Painter.

   Summarized:
   Peter Dutch, Math and chemistry
   Steven Writer, Dutch and chemistry
   Simon Painter, Dutch and history
   Karl English, Dutch and history.

2. Note that no two statements in the list can be true at the same time. Therefore, either 9 statements or 10 statements are false. However, if 10 statements were all false, then the last statement would be true, which is a contradiction. Thus, 9 statements were false. (The 9th statement is the only true one.)

3. The question that the traveller should ask is: *'Does the left road lead to London according to your brother?'* If the answer is 'Yes', the traveller should turn right, and if the answer is 'No', the traveller should turn left.

Explanation: There are four possible cases:

1. The traveller asks the question to the truth-telling brother, and the left road leads to London. The truth-telling brother knows that his lying brother would say that the left road does not lead to London, and so he answers 'No'.

2. The traveller asks the question to the truth-telling brother, and the right road leads to London. The truth-telling brother knows that his lying brother would say that the left road leads to London, and so he answers 'Yes'.

3. The traveller asks the question to the lying brother, and the left road leads to London. The lying brother knows that his truth-telling brother would say that the left road leads to London, and so he lies 'No'.

4. The traveller asks the question to the lying brother, and the right road leads to London. The lying brother knows that his truth-telling brother would say that the left road does not lead to London, and so he lies 'Yes'.

4. Draw the following as a family tree to understand it better. A is the grandfather of E, F and G, father of C and father-in-law of D.

B is the grandmother of E, F and G, Mother of C and mother-in-law of D.

C is the father of E, F and G, child of A and B and son of A and B.

D is the mother of E, F and G and daughter-in-law of A and B.

E is the child of C and D, grandchild of A and B and brother of F and G.

F is the child of C and D, daughter of C and D, grandchild

of A and B and sister of E and G.

G is the child of C and D, daughter of C and D, grandchild of A and B and sister of E and F.

Answer: At least 7 people are sitting at the table.

5. In this puzzle, you should *not* use your intuition, but let your common sense do the job: the chance that your first choice for a door was correct is 1/3; therefore, the chance that your first choice was wrong is 2/3.

The chance that one of the remaining doors is correct is also 2/3. With the help of the quizmaster (who knows which door hides the price, and thus is able to open one of the remaining doors which does not contain the price), you get to know which one of the remaining doors is incorrect. Now you also know which one of the remaining doors could be correct with a chance of 2/3!

Conclusion: You should switch doors, which doubles your chances!

For the disbelieving few: Consider the situation where there are 1000 doors instead of three. After you have chosen one door, the quizmaster points out 998 of the 999 doors that are left, that do not contain the prize. Should you switch to the other remaining door? Of course! If, out of 999 doors, the quizmaster (deliberately) leaves that door, chances are very large (999/1000) that it is the right one!

Exercise 2: Morse Code

1. What hath God wrought
2. Wheels on the bus
3. Meet at four pm
4. Look under the mat
5. Every cloud has a silver lining

Exercise 4: Word Wheels

1. Upswing, swing, swung, wings, swig, wigs, wing, wisp, wins.
2. Probate, boater, borate, rebato, abore, abort, bepat, boart, probe, rebop, taber, tabor, abet, bare, barp, bate, bear, beat, beta, boar, boat, boep, boet, bora, bore, bort, bota, brae, brat, prob.
3. Twelfth, theft, thelf, wheft, felt, fett, flew, heft, left, weft.
4. Buoyant, botany, bounty, atony, aunty, banty, bayou, bayau, bunty, bunya, noyau, outby, bayt, bony, buoy, toby, tony, tuny, yont, yuan.
5. Petrify, ferity, freity, fiery, freit, preif, refit, reify, rifte, rifty, treif, fier, fire, fret, frit, reft, reif, rife, rift, ryfe, terf, tref.
6. Housing, shogun, sough, suing, using, gnus, guns, hugs, huis, hung, huns, huso, nous, onus, shun, snug, sung, ughs, unis.
7. Voyager, avoyer, voyage, garvey, aygre, gayer, goary, gravy, ovary, yager, aery, ayre, eyra, gory, gray, grey, gyre, gyro, gyve, oary, orgy, oyer, vary, very, voar, yare, year, ygoe, yoga, yore.
8. Skimmer, kimmers, kermis, kimmer, merism, mimers, simmer, emirs, meris, merks, mikes, mimer, mimes, mires, mirks, miser, riems, smerk, smirk, emir, mems, meri, merk, mike, mime, mire, mirk, mirs, mise, rems, riem, rime, rims, semi, skim, smir.
9. Reptile, perlite, pelite, pelter, petrel, triple, leper, peril, peter, petre, piert, piler, plier, repel, tripe, leep, lept, lerp, lipe, peel, peer, pele, pelt, pere, peri, pert, pier, piet, pile, pirl, plie, pree, ripe, ript, trip.
10. Contort, cotton, croton, conto, roton, torot, tronc, coot, cott, nott, onto, oont, otto, ront, root, roto, toco, toon, toot, torc, torn, toro, tort, tron, trot.

Exercise 5: Figure It Out!

Kakuro

		6	3		2	1		2	1
	8	2	1		1	4		1	3
	9	3			4	2	1	3	5
		5	2	7	3		2	4	
			3	1					
		3	1	5	2			2	1
	1	2		3	1	2		8	3
	3	1			3	4	2	1	
						1	3		
		9	2		2	5	1	7	
	7	2	1	3	5			2	1
	2	1		2	1		1	3	2
	9	3		1	3		2	9	

WEEK 2—DAY 7

Exercise 2: Out-Of-The-Box Puzzles

1. This puzzle has no solution as a two dimensional puzzle.
   However, if you think of it as a three dimensional puzzle, the
   third house is connected to the electricity utility by digging
   a hole near the house and having the wire emerge through
   another hole near E.

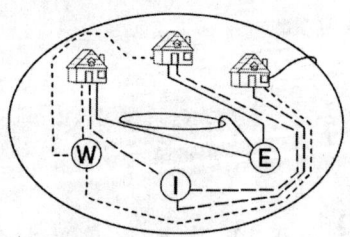

2.

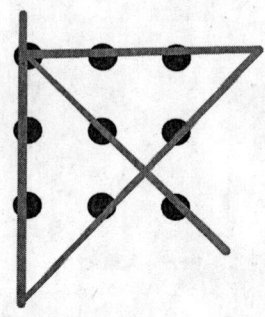

3. Place the letter Z in the third row so that the blank squares form the other omitted letter – T.

B	D	I	C	H	K
J				O	P
X	Z		A	G	Q
V	R		W	Y	U
S	E	N	M	F	L

4. His son. We can replace '*my father's son*' by '*myself*' since he is the only child. Now the riddle reads as '*This man's father is myself*', so 'this man' or the man in the painting is his son.

5. The man had the hiccups and wanted a glass of water to

help get rid of them. The bartender could hear the hiccups when the man spoke, so he brought the gun out to scare the hiccups away. It worked and the man thanked him and left happily, no longer needing the glass of water.

6. Anthony and Cleopatra were goldfish whose bowl was knocked over, perhaps by a clumsy dog.

7. The man pushing the car was a player in a monopoly game and his game piece was a car.

8. They all belonged to a snowman that had melted.

9. During a forest fire, a fire-fighting plane had scooped up some water from the lake to drop on the fire. The plane had accidentally picked up the unfortunate swimmer.

10. They were two of a set of triplets (or quadruplets etc.).

Appendix

The following is a list of games that train one or more cognitive skills in a fun way. These cognitive skills stimulate your brain which in turn leads to a healthy, agile brain. Some of these games are multiplayer games and some are games that you can play alone. This list is not exhaustive but gives you a good idea of how games can train your brain.

	Games	Cognitive Skill Trained
	Card Games	
1.	Solitaire	Planning, visualization, number sequencing
2.	Free Cell	Strategy, visualization, number sequencing
3.	Memory	Spatial, short-term, working memory
4.	Uno	Strategy, colour sequencing, social skills, tactics
5.	Euchre	Memory, tactics, communication
6.	Poker	Communication, perception, pattern recognition
7.	Dominion	Resource management, planning
8.	Snap!	Processing speed, motor movement, hand-eye coordination
9.	Canasta	Tactics, strategy
10.	Rummy	Counting, sequencing, pattern recognition
11.	Hearts / Donkey	Deductive reasoning, strategy
12.	Go fish	Deductive reasoning, pattern recognition
13.	Blackjack	Deductive reasoning, counting
14.	Set	Pattern recognition, processing speed,

	Board Games	
15.	Chess	Logic, active observation, pattern recognition, concentration, focus, spatial memory, problem-solving, processing speed, analytical, patience, working memory, procedural memory
16.	Battleship/ Sea Battle	Guessing, strategy, communication, deductive reasoning
17.	Boggle	Language, comprehension, creativity
18.	Candy Land	Colour recognition
19.	Reversi/ Othello	Strategy, spatial, observation
20.	Sorry	Counting, tactics, strategy
21.	Stratego	Strategy, tactics, memory
22.	Snakes and Ladders	Counting, observation
23.	Backgammon	Strategy, tactics, counting
24.	Pictionary	Social skills, communication, drawing, observation, perception,
25.	Chinese Checkers	Strategy, spatial, tactics
26.	Ludo	Tactics
27.	Guess Who?	Communication, language, social, deductive reasoning, problem solving
28.	Mouse Trap	Finger dexterity, processing speed, motor movements, hand-eye coordination
29.	Scrabble	Language, vocabulary, spelling, anagramming, strategy, counting
30.	Clue/Cluedo	Deductive reasoning, communication, social skills
31.	Monopoly and Business World	Negotiation, resource management, strategy, counting
32.	Draughts	Strategy, spatial memory, planning

33.	Hungry Hungry Hippos	Hand-eye coordination, processing speed, colour recognition
34.	Trivial Pursuit	Semantic memory, processing speed
35.	The Game of Life	Counting, reading
36.	Mastermind	Code cracking
37.	Carroms	Finger dexterity, fine motor movements, accuracy, procedural memory
	Blocks	
38.	Jenga	Manual dexterity, eye-hand coordination, precision, strategy, concentration, focus, spatial, problem-solving,
39.	Dominoes	Tactics, strategy, spatial memory, numerical reasoning
40.	Settlers of Catan	Resource management, negotiation, analytical skills, logic, strategy
41.	Pandemic	Decoding, numerical reasoning, logic, analytical skills
	Lego	Creativity, fine motor movements
	Puzzles	
42.	Word wheel, Word ladders, Word Pyramid, Hexalex	Language, comprehension, analytical, logical
43.	Minesweeper	Counting, spatial memory
44.	Word Search	Observation, processing speed
45.	Crossword	Language, comprehension
46.	Sudoku	Numerical reasoning, processing speed
47.	Kakuro	Numerical reasoning, processing speed
48.	KenKen/ Calcudoku/ Mathdoku/ KenDoku	Numerical reasoning, processing speed

49.	Jigsaw	Spatial, deductive reasoning
50.	Mancala	Observation, analytical, planning, strategy, problem-solving
51.	Tic Tac Toe	Problem-solving, spatial memory, pattern recognition
52.	Connect 4	Spatial memory, pattern recognition, sequencing
	Playground & Backyard Games	
53.	Hopscotch	Aim, physical flexibility, agility
54.	Duck Duck Goose	Processing speed, physical speed, agility
55.	Dodgeball	Aim, accuracy, processing speed, physical speed, agility
56.	Marbles	Aim, accuracy, finger dexterity, hand-eye coordination
57.	Croquet	Aim, accuracy, hand-eye coordination
58.	Hide & Seek	Intuition, speed
	Miscellaneous	
59.	Twister	Social skills, physical flexibility
60.	Rubik's Cube	Observation, pattern recognition, colour matching, concentration, focus, spatial memory, finger dexterity, problem-solving, eye-hand coordination, processing speed, visual, analytical, logical, patience
61.	Dungeons & Dragons	Role-playing, improvisation, tactics, numerical reasoning, creativity, imagination, lateral thinking, communication, social skills, comprehension
62.	Dumb charades	Non-verbal communication, observation, deductive reasoning, social skills
63.	Simon Says	Short-term memory, active observation

64.	20 Questions	Comprehension, language, analytical, deductive reasoning, social skills
65.	Mad Libs	Language, comprehension, social skills
66.	Brainvita	Finger dexterity, hand-eye coordination, focus, concentration

*Video games and console games have not been included in this list.

Bibliography

Katz, L.C., and Rubin, M. 2014. *Keep Your Brain Alive*. New York: Workman Publishing Company.

Gediman, C. L., and Crinella, F.M. 2005. *Brainfit: Curcuit Training for Your Mind and Your Memory*. Nashville, Tennessee: Thomas Nelson.

Scotts, J. (2013). *Exercise for the Brain: 70 Neurobic Exercises to Increase Mental Fitness & Prevent Memory Loss*. Speedy Publishing Books.

Jefferson, K. (2015). *Brain Training: 55 Techniques to Exercise Your Brain, Increase Your Brain Power and Improve Your Memory*. CreateSpace Independent Publishing Platform.

Jast, J. (2015). *Laser-Sharp Focus*. Amazon Digital Services LLC.

White, R. (2013). *Memory Improvement: How to Improve Your Memory in Just 30 Days*. Melrose, USA: Laurenzana Press.

O'Brien, T. (2016). *Game Time: Things You Ought to Know*. New Delhi: Rupa Publications India Pvt. Ltd.

Buzan, T. (2007). *Tony Buzan's Boost Your I.Q. and Sharpen Your Memory in Only 7 Days*. Hammersmith, London: Harper Element.

Bragdon, A. D., and Fellows, L. (2010). *Exercises for the Whole Brain*. New Delhi: Viva Books Pvt. Ltd.

Moore, G. (2006). *The 10 Minute Brain Workout*. London: Michael O'Mara Books Limited.

Reader's Digest (2000). *Reader's Digest Compendium of Puzzles & Brain Teasers*. London: The Reader's Digest Association Limited.

Websites

https://www.smithsonianmag.com
https://bebrainfit.com/brain-exercises/
http://www.csc.edu/learningcenter/study/memoryprinciples.csc
https://brilliant.org
https://puzzle.dse.nl
https://www.riddles.com
https://www.cognifit.com
https://www.mathplayground.com

Acknowledgements

Once again, a very special thank you to Yamini Chowdhury of Rupa Publications for the wonderful opportunity to write yet another book, the third, of this series. A huge thank you to the multi-talented Ritabrata Joardar for his beautiful illustrations. I would like to especially thank my husband Rabin Stephen, my daughters, Shifrah and Annika, and my parents, Reginald Solomon and Shantha Solomon, for their enduring love and support.